THE READING PLACE

Anthology of Award-winning Short Stories

ISBN-10: 0-9851833-2-2
ISBN-13: 978-0-9851833-2-5

DEDICATION

This anthology is dedicated to those who
know where the reading place is

To the authors featured in this book: Scribes Valley thanks you for
your time, patience, trust, and talent.

CONTENTS

THE READING PLACE
A Foreword by David L. Repsher, editor

We should all have one—a special place where we get away from the world. A place where distractions are kept to a minimum, worries and cares are forgotten, and an endless cornucopia of imagination is ours for the taking. A place where we can open a book, open our minds, and be transported elsewhere.

A reading place.

And that place could be anywhere: a soft bed in the bedroom, a cozy chair in the den, a cushy window seat, a lawn chair on the back porch, a single seat in a private bathroom, or even a booth in a crowded and noisy restaurant. It really doesn't matter where we read, as long as our minds can close off the world and focus on the words.

Within these pages are stories that can do just that. So take this book to your reading place, take a couple of deep breaths, open the cover, and begin reading.

Now...isn't that a great feeling?

FIRST PLACE

WHEN WE BECOME THE PHOTOGRAPHS
©2014 by Chelle Wotowiec

The woman with the blonde hair wiped tears from her cheeks before she came over to my bed. She didn't think I saw her crying and I wondered if this behavior was a part of her normal routine. She inched closer to the chair next to the bed, as if weights were strapped around her ankles, before she finally sat down and told me that Susan had passed. I watched the words escape her lips and I saw my reflection in her eyes.

The tone of this woman's voice, her wet cheeks, and puffy eyelids told me that I should know Susan. I'd dreamt a few nights before that my memories were stuck in my stomach. The children that I had, the house that I lived in, the career that I had once only dreamed of fulfilling; all of this was stuck in my stomach. Looking at this woman's questioning eyes, I hoped that if I sat up, pulled my body to a right angle, it would allow memories of Susan to surface.

Janet, the daytime nurse came into the room with clean sheets and my Aricept. She set the sheets on my end-table when she saw that my daughter was still here. She disappeared into the shared bathroom and came back out with a small plastic cup of water. I took the pills and right when I thought she was going to leave the room, she stopped short and said, "Wow, Maggie, this is the first time in days that you have sat up!" And then, as if her words had no consequence whatsoever, walked out of the room with her fake toothy smile.

"Are you okay, Mom?" She asked me after she placed her hand on mine.

I looked at her unfamiliar fingers and nodded my head. I'd pretend, I decided. Maybe it was a survival instinct—play the game. "I think so," I managed to say through my dry, cracked lips. "How did it happen?"

She was silent. I'd noticed the past few months that this woman had been putting on weight. Her upper arms had grown larger and her fingers fatter. She must have been in her forties, maybe fifties at the absolute latest. Her hair was disheveled, her blue blouse was wrinkled, and the skin on her face drooped. She cleared her throat and said, "You don't know how it happened?"

Her upper eyelids were beginning to swell even larger. This was going to be difficult, I was sure. I closed my eyes and thought very carefully of what to say next.

"Mom, answer me," she managed to spit out.

I kept my eyes closed. *Susan. Susan. Susan.* Then I was in my childhood bedroom with the powder-blue comforter and oak end-table. On the foot of the bed was my collie, Ginger, snoring. Ginger's leg was broken and wrapped in a cast as a result of a failed jump over the backyard fence. "She was sick," I said into the heavy room.

"Yes, Mom," the woman placed her hand on the back of my head and rubbed her fingers in a circular motion, "your youngest daughter was sick."

She dropped hints that I knew I had heard before. Susan was a single woman. She moved away at twenty-two and lived alone in downtown New York where she worked as a copy editor. She didn't call her sister often, but she called her mother all the time. She called me all the time, the woman told me. Susan decided at a young age never to have kids. This blonde-haired woman told me now that she never agreed with Susan's decision.

The woman continued to rub my head and when I remembered that I hadn't had my hair washed in over four days, I pulled my head away from her hand. Then she began to sob on my lap. I placed my hand on her back and let my fingers rest on her wrinkled blouse, just as I had seen the other women do with their children.

"Sssshh, now," I whispered as a mother would. I tried to imagine Susan, a woman that I created and a woman that grew inside of me, sick. It was something terminal, I was sure. She probably began to weaken. Maybe the first thing she noticed was a trembling hand or spotty vision. Before she knew it, it grew hard to breathe. Something as simple as breathing became a losing battle for her. As this sickness grew stronger, she probably shrank into her own skin and became nothing but bones. I pictured this but it didn't do anything for me. I didn't care about Susan.

The blonde woman sat up and pulled herself back together. Minutes went by and I looked at the curtain to my left that was supposed to be a wall. I had every wrinkle and every tear on the curtain memorized. I turned my head down to the right and focused on a small birthmark on this woman's neck. I placed my right pointer finger on it and closed my eyes. I tried to imagine bathing her as a child, placing the same finger on the same birthmark. I must have washed that pigmented skin a hundred times. I tried to picture wrapping up a young yellow-haired girl in a soft white bath towel.

I could hear Margie, the woman in the bed on the other side of that curtain, snoring. I was jealous of her. I wished I were sleeping too.

"Let's get out of here," the blonde woman said and picked up her purse. "Let's just do it, right now."

"What?" I reached for my blanket. Instead of finding my blanket, I found an old photo album. It was opened to a page displaying a faded photograph of a younger me with a child on my knee.

"Do you remember that, Mom?" She sat down on the bed next

to me and pulled the album onto her lap. She turned the page, "What about this one?"

The photograph showed two young girls sitting in adjoining mud puddles, smiling and waving at the camera.

"You took that one, Mom. You used a copy of this one in your portfolio. You said it caught something real about us that photographs rarely did."

She turned the page and we looked at more pictures of the two girls, the father, and myself. After she had turned through all of the pages, a photograph slipped out of the small sleeve of the back cover.

"I know him," I said. I brought the photograph closer to my eyes. It was much older than the rest, its corners torn. My father smiled at me in his brown suit and white necktie. A cigar smoked from his left hand. I closed my eyes and for a moment could smell his cologne.

The woman stood up off the bed and turned her face toward the door. She brought her right hand to her cheek. "You need fresh air, Mom." She used a tissue she pulled out of her purse. "You're not supposed to be here. No one is supposed to be here."

* * *

I followed the blonde woman down the corridor, through the doors past the lounge, and out into the parking lot. As I took in the seventy-degree air, I remembered the country sky of my childhood. I grew up with only a father, as my mother had passed during childbirth. I had only known her through faded photographs kept inside an armoire.

Another breath of that air and I realized that I didn't even know what month it was. In fact, I could have sworn it was near Christmastime. I knew this because that was the time when all of the other patients—or residents—cried the most. There had been a lot of crying lately.

Margie, for one, has been saying that she is dying. She says that her body is expiring and there is nothing she can do about it. She'd heard about the three-year life expectancy once you're checked into one of these places. She is over halfway through her second year. She asks me how long I have been here before she came and I tell her I don't know. I try really hard to remember, but time doesn't seem to work the same anymore, I tell her over and over again. A day is no longer twenty-four hours.

Margie tells me about her life before she was diagnosed with Alzheimer's and it sounds like a good one. She says that it's harder having a good one because it's that much harder to watch it slip away. I try to tell her that it isn't slipping as much as it is fading, and there is a difference.

I knew it was a Tuesday because Tuesdays were when this lady came to visit. "It is summertime?" I asked.

The blonde-haired woman paused and looked back at me, puzzled. We both stood frozen in our tracks and I noticed that my legs were shaking. "Of course it is summertime. We're into September already."

"Oh, okay," I said and waited for her to pick up her step.

She led the way to a blue Ford Escort. I knew the car when I opened the backdoor and slowly slid onto the leather seat. I knew the pattern and the cigarette burns on the roof's upholstery.

"Don't you want to sit up front?"

I had already closed the door. "I'm fine."

There was a silence and I waited for her to start the car.

"Mom, are you okay?" the woman asked as she finally closed the driver's side door. I looked at her closely from this angle. I looked at her cheekbones and the way her lips met the skin that met her nose. Still did not recognize her.

"I remember when Susan called me seven years ago and told me her diagnosis. I remember the hardness in her voice and how for the first time it sounded closer to home. It wasn't a voice that was planted eight hundred miles away."

Again I tried to remember and again there was nothing.

"Her voice was sitting right next to me, next to *us*. I remember the blue nightgown you were wearing and how the flowers across your body seemed placed without rhyme or reason. I can still see your body collapsing onto the hardwood floor of my dining room and the sound of your wail. You *wailed,* Mom. Don't you remember that?"

There was a silence as I watched a woman with her two children get out of a car a few feet away. I wondered who they were visiting.

"Mom?"

"I just—I'm not sure I should leave here."

We both continued to sit in silence.

"Do you not want to leave here?" She turned her body toward me.

I looked down at the old hands with tissue-paper skin on my lap. I wondered when they had grown so old. "Where will I go?" I asked barely above a whisper.

The woman cleared her throat. "Home. Mom, you will go home." The woman turned back around and placed both of her arms on the steering wheel. She sighed and then ran her right hand through her knotty hair. "We talked about this last week."

"I—I don't—"

"Mom," her voice cracked, "I need you to *try.* Do you understand that?" She continued to look out the window. "Don't you get it? You're going to *die* here!" She stepped out into the parking lot and slammed the door. I watched her crumple down to her knees. After a few minutes she sat down on the pavement and leaned against the back passenger door.

I rolled the window down.

"You don't know where your home is, do you?"

I was silent.

After a long while she finally stood up. She opened the back passenger door and said, "Come on, Mom, let's go back." She smiled as I gave her my arm.

Once outside, the air reminded me of the air my father and I breathed on a July evening. We sat on the dock he'd built out back and let our feet rest in the cold water while Ginger swam in the lake. Her leg had healed by then, but she was left with a permanent limp. My father said she liked to swim because it made her forget that she was handicapped. Then he was quiet, letting the word *handicapped* sink into our skin. My father then cleared his throat and told me of the war. He told me that it was one thing to kill a man in self-defense and it was a whole other thing to kill a man for a cause that, when it was all said and done, just didn't add up. He told me of Johnny, the best man he met over there, and how he came back with nothing but a head and a torso. My father stopped and he cried, and I didn't remind him that he had told me this story before.

About the author:

Chelle Wotowiec, 27, teaches college level English in Phoenix, Arizona.

She no longer waits tables, but has not been able to entirely shed that monthly nightmare where more and more people join the booth and demand drinks and, as it turns out, she does not have her pen in hand.

Originally from Ohio, she is currently going where ever the flow takes her. The flow of what, she is not sure.

She misses her mother, father, sister, grandparents, Ripley, and her good friend Nate. Homesick has taken on a new definition now that 2,000 miles of earth separate her from them all.

If there is a meaning to life, she is pretty sure that cats are part of the equation. She also thinks that if you have not loved a cat, you have never really known a cat.

She believes there is no greater power than the power of language.

Words will change the world.

SECOND PLACE

TO ENDURE

©2014 by Drew Hardman

Every crack in the boardwalk sent a furious bolt of pain through her bones. The burn seemed to radiate up from her twisted little feet, stopping for a gulp of gasoline at each joint: ankles, knees, hips, shoulders, elbows, wrists, and back down the track. This type of pain, the bump-and-bruise type, was sharp and growing sharper every day. But it was temporary, and she preferred it immensely over the steady ache that had settled into her legs in increments over a thirty-year lease. The jolt of the boardwalk was like the thin thread of icing on the edge of a dense cake, which had grown over the years from a dainty cupcake to a massive, multi-layered monstrosity.

Anne tried to focus her mind on the beauty of the ocean stretching across the horizon, alight with the late morning sun. It was a view she could appreciate from the deck of the beachfront rental. A view she had, in fact, appreciated each and every day of their week-long vacation, which would come to a close tomorrow morning.

She shared that serene view from the perfect little sun deck with a cigarette and a vodka or two. The smell of tobacco blended with the complex, briny bouquet of the Atlantic Ocean, calling to mind some of the best memories of her waning life. Her daughters came and went, chatting as they cooked at the grill or refreshed her drink, and she marveled at the wonderful and complete women they had become. She saw Mac's genial face in theirs and his flaxen curls in their sun-bleached and wind-combed hair.

Mostly, though, she saw Mac in the happy and laughing faces of her grandsons, all five of them. She especially loved to share her view of the Atlantic with those wonderful boys. They were respectful, each in his own way, and they made time out of their fun-filled days to sit with Grammy—as they called her—telling her about school or sports or anything. But it was best when they forgot she was there and went about their adolescent business: throwing pizza crusts for the eager seagulls, counting their quarters to spend on video games at the boardwalk arcade, and trading baseball cards on the patio table, weighing their options with a calculated, no-nonsense air.

Anne thought that her husband had been a child, even in his later years, and she wondered sometimes if she had ever really appreciated his innocence, his good nature and his ready laugh, like she appreciated the reflection of him she saw in her grandsons. She thought that probably she had, but even those distant years were clouded with the pain that would chase her to the grave.

Sometimes, when the pain had started her drinking a little early, she lost herself on that perfect little sun deck amidst the noise of her family and the ocean, the smells, the sights. When she turned her stiff neck, she saw Mac there at the chair next to her, his chin resting in his hands to frame a broad smile. His own cocktail was stationed by one elbow, the glass sweating in the hot sun. Sometimes Anne could even hear his sweet voice mixed with the rest, singing a piece of the "Star-Spangled Banner" or recounting an afternoon of mackerel fishing.

It was a chore not to grow sullen when she thought of her husband there, but she did the very best she could. When it was too painful to be around her daughters and her grandsons, she hobbled away on the cane to the big room where they put her, near the bathroom and the kitchen. She lay with her swollen knees bent painfully and tried to sleep. Mostly, though, she sipped her vodka and remembered.

Painful as they were, Anne enjoyed these treks to the Jersey shore. Soon enough, her grandsons would be in college, spread about the country and starting lives of their own. They would eventually be too busy to spare a week to gather at the shore with Grammy. Family vacations, she knew, were most cherished by the very young and the very old, those few that cannot surrender the effort to worry about the future.

But it was not enough to spend her week cooped-up on the top floor of their quaint rental home. Despite near-constant admonition from the other adults, she had made her annual request to journey down the stairs one day in advance to visit the sandy white beach she so appreciated from her spot on the deck. The trip would cost her dearly, she knew. A fare she paid with real pain.

Anne clenched her weak hands along the PVC rails of the wheelchair as the absurd orange wheels bumped their way through another gap in the boardwalk. From behind, her youngest daughter gave her shoulder a light squeeze. As always, they had rented a beach wheelchair, equipped with its own pink and white umbrella. The ridiculous contraption sported oversized rubber wheels in construction-cone orange that could be pushed, with some effort, along the loose sand at the edge of the beach. Anne thought of the silly chair as a big wheel tricycle for grandmas.

She hated the big wheel with a passion. It was not so much the substantial pain it caused, though that was certainly something to consider. Even with an extra layer of padding, the big wheel delivered every bounce and jounce like a lightning rod to her bones. What she really hated, though, was the pity it roused. Its bulk and bright colors invited the worst kinds of stares from the families along the beach. Every second on the wheelchair was a dagger to her dignity. But she endured.

They came finally to a long ramp that provided access to the sand. The daughter traded positions with the son-in-law for the final leg of the journey, but it was still tough going. With a firm hand, he guided the big wheel in and around the dunes, taking every measure to keep the wheelchair steady. Nonetheless, the big wheel swayed back and forth in the uneven, loose sand. It was everything she could do to keep from crying out against the rocking and the stopping and going.

As they neared the tide line, the sand grew even and firm, packed hard with moisture. Anne made herself relax the tension from her aching arms and legs, and the vibrant towels and swimsuit-clad beachgoers proved an excellent distraction. She delighted in the crash and sigh of the waves—a sound she could not quite grasp from the deck of the rental house.

Anne finally eyed a knot of boys that she instantly recognized as her own. They were crowded some ways apart from where their parents had settled with their towels and beach chairs and coolers. She gave a little chuckle and pointed towards the boys, but her son-in-law had already set the course, following his own curiosity.

As they wheeled closer, the boys looked up and called to her. Their young eyes held none of the pity she saw on her daughter's face, and Anne loved them all the more for it. They ran to her, the youngest giving her a painful hug around the shoulders. They each wore a brightly-colored pair of swimming trunks with smears of sunscreen blotching their bare chests and freckled faces.

Around them, she could see evidence of the day's adventures. The beginnings of a sloppy sandcastle waited for the coming tide, its half-finished moat littered with cheap beach toys and a foam football. In their excitement, the boys directed her attention to the latest object of their youthful attention. It was a jellyfish, she saw, or what was left of one. Its iridescent shape glittered in the sun, appearing a translucent silver in places and a deep maroon in others.

Once more they gathered around their prize, peering at the jellyfish with a look of both wonder and mischief that only young boys can master. One of them poked at the remains with a plastic shovel, spurring a chorus of laughter and groans of "eww." It was a familiar scene, and she could not help but smile.

* * *

The boys lay in a line along the edge of the concrete dock, their heads peering over the side of the structure and into the shallow green water below. There were four of them here. Her fifth and final grandson would not be born for another two years. From her perch high above the dock, Anne could hear them discussing tactics for catching a crayfish, which was—in their view—a very serious business.

The little crustaceans flocked to the remains of this morning's trout catch, expertly filleted by her son-in-law. Discarded in the shallow water along the dock, the glittering rainbow scales drew the crayfish from their camouflage along the rocky creek bed, and the boys watched them with wonder, their little hands hovering anxiously just above the water. They were deciding on the best approach to pinch the crayfish by their tails before the finger-length creatures had the chance to pinch back. Crayfish, of course, made the very best fishing bait.

Anne reclined in her straight-backed rocking chair on the screened porch. The view from the porch showed Slippery Rock Creek in all its glory. Despite its shallow depth, the stream spanned nearly fifty yards across, and she thought that here, at least, the Slippery Rock was more a river than a creek.

Immense pine trees arched out over the water, stretching desperately for a glint of sun in the murky Western Pennsylvania forest. The smell of pine was fresh on the air, braided subtlety with the sharp, clean smell of spring water over dead leaves and the all-too-familiar scent of tobacco.

The Slippery Rock was a symphony of stirring noises. A dozen species of birds called this part of the stream home, chiefly among them the honking Canadian Geese who sailed periodically over their heads. Across the creek, she could hear a woodpecker knocking furiously at a tree and the occasional croak of a bullfrog from the bank. Behind it all was the constant gurgling of the ground spring that fed the cabin's plumbing and the distant rush of whitewater downstream.

Across from her, Mac sat sipping at a Budweiser and shouting words of encouragement down at the boys. His cheeks held that familiar rosy flush that she saw already on the faces of her young grandsons. He shot her a wink as one of the boys braved a grasp at a crayfish, only to draw his hand back with a splash.

She smiled back at Mac, shifting her weight around to get a better look at the boys. The movement sparked a bolt of pain in her hip, and she stifled a grimace. She took a long drink, noticing—not for the first time—the ugly lumps that had taken shape on her wrist and her knuckles. Anne wondered what would happen when she could no longer grip the cane, but she thought she knew the answer.

Anne was still recovering from her walk down to the cabin the day before. As always, she and Mac had arrived earlier than the others, driving the meager half-hour from their home in Pittsburgh to ready camp for the rest of the family. The last leg of the journey took them a mile or so over rough gravel road, which set her joints to aching almost immediately. The worst, though, was the path.

Mac had parked their station wagon at a turnaround overlooking the cabin and the dock below. Access to the cabin itself required a hike down a meandering earthen path no longer than the creek was wide. Over the years, Mac had tampered the trail down to a gentle slope, lining the path with smooth rocks from the river, but despite his best efforts, the path down to the cabin proved an especially difficult challenge to a woman suffering from rheumatoid arthritis.

As always, he had rounded their modest vehicle to open her door, offering her the cane from the backseat. As he set about unpacking their groceries and clothes, she had struggled painfully to her feet. Without a word, Mac set off down the path, carrying everything but his wife herself.

Anne followed along dutifully, taking great effort to pick and choose her steps on the rocky path. Every minute shift of the soil and gravel threatened to topple her small frame. It took her thirty minutes to traverse the same path that her grandsons bounded down in thirty seconds. When she arrived at the cabin, Mac was waiting on the porch. He had prepared her cocktail himself and sat fidgeting with the radio dials to find the baseball game.

Her daughters considered this ritual cold and heartless, and maybe it was. The path, after all, was gentle enough for a wheelchair. They could not understand how their father could ever put the woman he loved through that kind of torment.

But in all their fifty years of marriage and through hundreds of trips to the cabin, Anne had never so much as mentioned the harrowing walk down the path to Mac. It was never an issue. She thought Mac understood her disease in a way that her daughters never could, or perhaps they just didn't want to. He understood that her affliction—her cross to bear—would never kill her, like the cancer that took him from this world. It would make her suffer, worse and worse each day. It would maim her and ruin her over time. But it would not kill her.

He understood that the day she was beaten by the path may well mark the last time she ever attempted it—the beginning of the wheelchair and the end of her mobility. He made her take the path—let her take the path—to show her that she could.

And for whatever reason, she took a kind of silly pride in her walks up and down that path. She thought that maybe he did too.

* * *

They took a family picture there on the beach, with everyone gathered around Grammy's dreadful wheelchair. She asked her daughter to remove the gaudy umbrella, saving at least a scrap of her dignity. The boys went about their play and the adults returned to their books, while Anne watched the ocean lap at the sand from under a floppy straw hat.

As the morning turned to afternoon she bought the boys ice

cream from the Mister Softee cart that passed by along the boardwalk, declining their offer for a cone or a Popsicle. She watched them jog up the beach to join the rest of the children in line. When they returned with her change, she made them keep it for the arcade.

What she wanted then—needed really—was a drink. It was past cocktail hour, which had slid mournfully up and up over the last few years, from a respectful 7:00 p.m. to those shameful early afternoons. She remembered the words from the very first therapist who tried to address the alcohol, a young woman who said everything with a little smile. That smile always seemed to take the sincerity out of her words. Maybe that was why Anne remembered them.

"Arthritis is a study of pain," she said, no doubt quoting some professor or respected text. "It's a study of pain and the way you cope with it. And the way you're coping with it, Anne, is the wrong way."

The wrong way? Yes, Anne knew that alcohol was a depressant—right up there with chronic pain, eh? And yes, Anne knew that the aftereffects of alcohol leave the body chemistry in all sorts of disarray, which can often lead to anxiety—both the mental and the physical variety. She knew all of that firsthand.

She also knew the kind of ugly pattern that anxiety and depression can paint on a person's will, like the miniature whirlpools in the rapids or the pull of the riptide under the surf. Anxiety leads to depression. Depression leads to anxiety. And the pain just keeps on coming with the current, worse and worse for every minute that she bears it. *Have a drink*, it begs. And she concedes.

Taking all of that into account, Anne thought she was managing as well as could be expected. She was, after all, on vacation with her family. She was on the beach for goodness sake. The wrong way? No, she thought it was more like a detour, and all roads lead to Rome, even the winding paths and the boardwalks.

Her distracted mind again sought the tranquility of the

Atlantic. Beyond the shallow breakers, the water was an earnest blue, still and peaceful despite the breeze that caught the corners of the towels and tugged at her hat. She made her decision then and there, struggling for a moment to kick away her cheap Keds slip-on sneakers, still a bright white despite their age. With a grimace, she leaned forward in the big wheel and plunged her bare feet into the hot sand, clenching her toes despite the ache. It felt as wonderful as ever.

With a wave, she brought her eldest grandson to her side. He towered over her in the wheelchair, but his boyish face still held a trace of the baby fat that she knew would burn away in the coming year. Anne held one arm out, and the boy took it obediently, asking if everything was okay. She surprised him by struggling to her feet, pulling heavily on his sturdy frame.

If arthritis was a study of pain, standing up from a sitting position was worth a credit or two, Anne thought. The anguish must have shown on her face, because she was soon surrounded by eager helpers, the adults anxious for her to sit back down.

Instead, Anne took a step forward, relying on her grandson as she did her trusty cane. One of her daughters took her other arm, and together they made another annual pilgrimage from the beach to the surf. She knew the rest of them were following in an embarrassing little procession, but she didn't bother to look. Every step was pain. But every step also brought a fresh sensation to her bare feet. The hot sand gave way to cool and then wet, squishing soothingly between her toes and along her heels. And then they were in the water—a rewarding rush of ice flooding up to her gnarled ankles.

The stunted leftovers of a wave came charging past, sending a splash of salt water up the legs of her khaki capris. Anne closed her eyes and relished the tug of the water as it retreated back towards the surf, chipping away at the sand below her feet to create size-seven pillars in the surf—the crumbling foundations of an old woman. The next little breaker started the process anew, and she wondered if the meager pull of the waves would be enough to wrench her ninety-five pounds out to sea. But her helpers kept her upright.

When Anne opened her eyes again, she found to her delight that her other grandsons had abandoned their vigil. They were scattered about the surf, searching intently for broken pieces of sand dollars and other flotsam. For once she was relieved to find the big wheel stationed silently behind her legs, and she eased herself into the chair with all the grace her tired body could muster.

She spent another few moments watching the boys while the water surged around her stiff legs, occasionally catching the big wheel just right to spray her face and shoulders with a fine mist. When her daughter suggested it was time to return, Anne did not protest, but she was in no hurry. She felt the need for a drink but not the want—not yet. She waited contentedly as the others retrieved their sandals and packed their bags.

Then they wheeled her back through the rough dunes and the rutted boardwalk and towards the grueling walk up the stairs, where she would wait with her cigarettes and her vodka for tomorrow.

About the author:

A former journalist turned copywriter, Drew Hardman is a marketing communications specialist and freelance writer based in Pittsburgh, Pa. With published works ranging from news and sports features to substantive legal articles, case studies, and short fiction, his portfolio includes interviews with Grammy-nominated artists, documentary film makers, and subject matter experts representing any number of industries. He is a two-time W.Va. Press Association award winner, and his fiction has received honors on The Renegade Word and WritersType.

THIRD PLACE

WAR OF THE WORLD'S FAIR
©2014 by Mike Tuohy

The cool May drizzle only made me pedal harder, even where I could coast. Pooky tires and a bent frame would not slow this fourth-grader down. I had a date with the Future.

The old yellow buses lined up like boxcars in front of Washington Elementary. Though still covered with the road grime of the New Jersey winter, they emitted a warm glow of promise. Eager to get a closer look, I shoved my bike amongst the others in the crowded rack and trotted across the squishy, greening lawn.

Hand-lettered placards bearing the letters WF taped to the driver's side windows made it official. These fine coaches would soon bear the entire fourth grade class, at least those with permission slips, to the 1964 New York World's Fair. Nothing but a nuclear attack would stop it. If the Russkies would hold off one more day, I could die happy, fulfilled in every way a nine-year-old boy could imagine, except maybe for driving a car or flying with a jetpack.

I wanted to climb on board and claim a window seat, but my instructions were specific. Failure to be in Miss Dixon's classroom before the first bell would mean getting left behind. I dared not take a chance. With a head filled with visions of futuristic architecture with spires, curves, and odd geometries, I reluctantly entered the stodgy old school building. With its dull red brick walls, slate-hipped roof, and sash windows, it felt like stepping into the past. Not where I wanted to be.

Yellow triangles on a circle of black identified the building as a fallout shelter. Solid as the walls appeared, the gaping windows worried me during our "duck and cover" drills. At an assembly the previous fall, we enjoyed a Civil Defense film including footage of actual atomic tests. A home composed of the same suburban substances that housed us all swayed one way from the blast then back the other in the suction of the rising mushroom cloud. Some kids had nightmares and were afraid to come to school. Counselors came to lead class discussions about nuclear war a week later.

Asked my reaction to the movie, I shared my personal vision wherein the initial shock wave would shower us all with shards of glass, momentarily sticking out like porcupine quills until the nuclear fireball reached us, melting the shards and leaving our smoking, meatless bones bedecked with little rhinestones. That scenario won me an appointment with a bald and bearded pipe-smoking doctor in the principal's office.

When a far-off presidential assassination interrupted the session, the adults suddenly seemed to share my point of view. Lacking any better idea, the principal sent us all home early to await the bright flashes in the relative safety of our basements. The black and white television spewed nothing but bad news from grim announcers for days. My cartoon favorites went on vacation. Nineteen sixty-three ended badly.

My fascination with apocalyptic visions faded as the opening of the World's Fair approached. The rising towers of the New York pavilion and the skeletal globe of the Unisphere tantalized me each time my family visited my grandmother on Long Island. Soon, I would be up close to these wonders, provided Khrushchev kept his finger off the button for the rest of the day. I took the stairs two at a time and put dismal thoughts aside with each step. I *will* walk on the moon. I *will* have a flying car. Science *will* find a cure for freckles.

At the top, I had an epiphany. The World's Fair was, after all, the fair of the Whole Wide World. The U.S.S.R. had to have a pavilion there. Surely, they would not drop an A-bomb on their own exhibit, no matter how crappy and full of propaganda it might be. It naturally followed that Flushing Meadows would be the safest place on the planet, at least for a while. Buoyed by the perfection of this logic, I put aside thoughts of annihilation and ran down the hall to my classroom.

First bell came at 8:50 and the hallway clock read 8:30. To my amazement, all my classmates were already there when I walked in. Eddie Elphick, the closest thing I had to a best friend, grinned like a sleep-deprived maniac. "Hey, Jackson! You're late."

I had not slept more than a couple of hours myself, and then only just before dawn. It was a deep sleep and I awoke in a panic, thinking I missed the field trip. "Am not! Teacher's not even here."

"Miss Dixon just went out to check on our bus." He rabbit-punched my shoulder. "You better not make me miss the *Futurama*. All the sixth-graders say it's the coolest thing in the world."

I resisted my normal inclination to dispute just about anything Eddie said. He echoed the opinion of my brother, a ninth grader of some credibility. I still had to confront him. "So why don't we just do that one all stinkin' day?"

Unfazed by my sarcasm, Eddie punched my shoulder. "Don't be a stooge. We gotta go see the Johnson Wax pavilion." He pointed to the souvenir map his grandma gave him. "See? It looks like a flying saucer."

"My brother says they just show you a stupid movie."

"Yeah, but you get to go inside. It's built like a spaceship!"

It looked cool, but so did the Pepsi pavilion and it was full of singing dolls. I could see in Eddie's face that our continued friendship might well depend on our going to the Johnson Wax exhibit. How bad could a movie be? "Okay. We'll probably need to sit down for a while."

Our classmate Kevin Bryson would not be sitting down. A human dynamo, he seemed driven to share his abundant energy and enthusiasm with the world. There being no adult supervision, he grabbed the forbidden hook-pole and proceeded to unlatch and open the row of massive windows overlooking the playground. He shouted down at a group of third-graders engaged in a game of Red Rover despite the intermittent rain. "Hey! While you babies are playing kickball at recess, we're gonna be riding a monorail!"

A chorus of indecipherable gibberish, rich with outrage and envy, arose from below.

Miss Dixon arrived with little impact on the hubbub. "Now, Kevin, you are not supposed to open the windows without permission."

Kevin lowered his gaze to the floor, obediently handed over the pole, and went to his desk. Miss Dixon set about pulling the windows back down while he sat quietly to my right; hands folded, eyes fixed on the blackboard. If he did more than blink during the next five minutes, I couldn't tell it.

Kevin spent the prior year and the year before that in Mrs. Coffen's third grade class. Though spared the experience, I heard enough about her to make me appreciate being assigned to Mrs. Larsen, a sweet lady who really wanted us to learn multiplication.

Mrs. Coffen wanted her students to learn the rules. Though corporal punishment had long since ceased in our public schools, there seemed to be no official policy regarding psychological torture. Her reputation for bringing tough guys to tears left few who dared risk humiliation in front of their classmates.

Miss Dixon was more like a young version of Mrs. Larson but with some distinctions. Red hair instead of blue. Freckles instead of wrinkles. Tight skirt that hugged her like paint on a bowling pin instead of a loose dress that left one wondering if the old lady had legs at all. They both used plenty of rouge, but only on Miss Dixon did it seem to serve a purpose.

When Miss Dixon smiled, leaned forward and rang her little hand bell, it was like the song of the ice cream truck. We all quieted down. "Class, I need to go back down and get the roster. I am counting on you to be on your best behavior while I'm gone. If there is any problem, Mrs. Coffen is just two doors away. She knows to check in on you."

Kevin visibly shuddered at the sound of the name. I tensed a little myself as I pictured her coming down the hall with her rubber-tipped pointer at the ready, dark hair pulled back and tied up like a captive animal. Her sharp nose, pointed chin—but most of all the dark eyebrows against pale skin—worked together to project a constant dissatisfaction. Then there was her voice: hard, clipped, and accusing. None of us wanted to deal with that.

Eddie's hand shot up but he wasn't waiting to be called upon. "Will the buses have a police escort?"

Miss Dixon, well accustomed to such idiocy from Eddie, smiled sweetly. "I'll look into it." She left and we all stayed in our desks, watching as the second hand on the wall clock slowed as if to torment us.

Kevin had been sitting upright and absolutely still for longer than I had ever seen. It seemed that eight minutes was his limit. With no warning, he bolted from his desk and headed for the hook-pole. He had more to share with the kids outside and only a few minutes to do so. Within seconds, he had all five windows up and a dozen companions taunting the third graders with the usual insults, many of which involved substitution of "turd" for "third". A squadron of paper aircraft followed, some bearing messages of mock pity for all the "little babies" who would have to stay behind while we went to the greatest event ever to take place on Planet Earth.

When words and propaganda ceased having an impact, Kevin upped the ante. "Hey! You can use this for hop-scotch!" With that, he pitched a long piece of blackboard chalk.

It hit a kid on the back of the head. He turned around and shook his fist. "I'm telling Teddy!"

I recognized him as Scott Nelson. Teddy, his brother, was a sixth grader already fond of picking on Kevin.

Kevin was unperturbed. "Why don't you just write it down?" He launched a handful of chalk all at once. It shattered at Scott's feet. All the guys at the window opened up with chalk of various colors, sending the third-graders into retreat and leaving a semi-circle of pastel points that spread and merged on the wet pavement as the rain briefly picked up, leaving only the more stalwart students, mostly boys.

Having exhausted the supply of chalk, we scrambled for more ammunition, commandeering gum erasers, crayons and modeling clay for the war effort. The playground below our classroom soon turned festive with colorful detritus. Each time the third-graders moved in to return fire, we drove them back with something new.

Whenever we played Army after school, Eddie adopted the role of 'Sarge.' He considered himself a natural leader and he fell into character right away. "Okay, Jackson! Stand guard at the door. Let us know the second anybody starts coming this way."

Much as I wanted to join in the fusillade, I obeyed, but not without a condition. "I'll do two minutes watch duty, then you have to relieve me."

Eddie pressed his lips together and gave a single nod. "You got it, soldier."

I stood with one foot propping the door open and divided my attention among the clock on the wall, the hallway and the chaos by the window. It was tough staying out of the fray but I was heartened that it sounded like our side was winning. The rising noise level, both within our room and that coming from outside, was sure to catch the attention of Mrs. Coffen. Her sense of hearing was legendary. She could hear gum, contraband in her class, being unwrapped six desks back.

At ten minutes to nine, my shift up, Eddie remained by the window, pulling large hunks from a ball of modeling clay and tossing them sidearm at the enemy. He ignored my pleas until out of ammo and only then came to my side. I only had four minutes before the first bell, when the playground would start to clear.

"Jeez, Eddie! Don't I get a turn?"

He grinned. "Sorry, soldier. I had them on the run."

"Screw you." I took off for the front, scanning the floor and desks for munitions. The only loose items left on Miss Dixon's desk were a stapler, a tape dispenser and a dictionary. Those were definitely off-limits. The only thing left on the floor was an empty metal trashcan. I grabbed it.

Having only one shot at glory, I hoisted my payload and tried to shove it through an open window. Slightly tapered, the lower, narrower end, slid out with little effort but the last six inches was of a greater diameter than the space below the sash. I pushed down on the lip of the container. It gave a little, but not enough to do anything but wedge it in tighter.

Eddie called out from his post. "Cheese it! Coffen's coming."

Kevin was by my side, laughing as we struggled to push the container through. At the sound of his old teacher's name, his face went slack and he retreated to his desk.

Eddie rushed over and began slamming windows down. When he got to me, he put all his weight with mine and pushed down. The metal gave just enough and the trashcan popped into the outside air, tumbling as it fell. Eddie pulled the window down just as the payload impacted with a hollow, metallic thud.

With everything closed up and everyone seated, we followed Kevin's example.

Two minutes before the first bell, Mrs. Coffen stepped through the door, pointer in hand. This was reputed to be a 'James Bond' type of device, equipped with interchangeable tips for inflicting pain on boys in a variety of ways. We all stared straight ahead and forced a group "Good morning, Mrs. Coffen." The windows were shut, the room clean, and the students quiet.

Not easily fooled, the terror of the third grade clearly knew something was amiss. Her measured pace brought her to a halt a few feet from the weakest link. Kevin was un-naturally still but blinking furiously.

Shifting only my eyes, I tracked Mrs. Coffen as she surveyed the room. I tried to anticipate what might catch her attention. The chalk tray was suspiciously empty, but I knew that, unlike Miss Dixon, she gathered and stowed hers at the end of each day. The desktops were oddly free of any stray materials, as was the floor. She still did not know that every available scrap of paper had exited the window in some wadded or folded form. We cleaned house.

Mrs. Coffen walked slowly over to Miss Dixon's desk, casting a controlling glance back at the class every few seconds. It had to be killing her that twenty-three fourth-graders were sitting quietly at their desks with no adult supervision. The very concept undermined her worldview. She looked up at the ceiling. Not a single pencil jammed in the acoustic tile. She examined the cloakroom and cubbies. No contraband there. "Well, it seems Miss Dixon has taught you well on matters of tidiness."

A few of the girls giggled. I bit my lip. We had committed the perfect crime.

Not yet through, Mrs. Coffen walked around the teacher's desk. Then drew herself upright and directed her pointer. "Kevin! Where is the wastebasket?"

Kevin started to turn in his seat to face me. Was he looking for help or was he going to rat me out? Before he could speak, something struck a pane with a muffled thud. I surmised blackboard eraser. A sharp *tik* followed. Probably chalk. Soon, a steady rain of small objects tapped and thudded against the glass, some leaving colorful marks, some sticking. Crayons, rubber erasers and modeling clay continued in an incriminating hailstorm while Mrs. Coffen regarded us all with a look that said, "There will be consequences," her trademark phrase.

The five-minutes-to-class bell rang and the barrage ceased. With one shaking index finger, Mrs. Coffen slowly traced an arc in the air. "You students will remain in your seats and stay quiet until I return with your teacher and the principal. Understand?"

We mumbled our assent and bent our necks as in prayer.

This was apparently not enough. "Do you understand me, Kevin?"

Were it not for the support of his desk, I was sure Kevin would have collapsed and drawn himself into a fetal position. His only audible reaction consisted of an expulsion of gas that rose to a high squeak and fell away like a dying bird. He buried his face in his hands and shook as if silently sobbing.

Mrs. Coffen stepped back, her finger still raised, defying any response from the rest of us. Amazingly, nobody laughed, not even Eddie Elphick, a guy who regarded fart noises the most irresistible form of humor. After five full seconds of silence, she turned on one heel and left.

With the racket of all the other kids rushing to class we did not have to stay quiet, but we did. There was nothing anyone wanted to either hear or say. When the final bell rang, we resigned ourselves to another day of mind-numbing school activities. Fractions. Verbs. State capitals.

A poster on the bulletin board, featuring the Unisphere, the symbol of the 1964 World's Fair, mocked me. I had the sensation of flinging from its orbit into deep space. There would be no *Futurama*, no robot Lincoln, no monorail, not even the crummy Johnson Wax pavilion. Life would not be worth living.

Not a minute after Mrs. Coffen left the room, Kevin bolted for the hook pole. Instead of opening windows, he headed for the door. Several thoughts occurred to me. Perhaps he had murder on his mind. Maybe, if I saved Mrs. Coffen, I could still go to the Fair. Certainly, if I stayed at my desk, I would miss out either way.

Out in the hallway, I found Kevin pressing the tip of the pole against the glass rod of a fire alarm. He could have reached it with his fingers but he wielded the pole with a ceremonial flourish that somehow elevated his action from simple mischief to pure glory.

With the alarm echoing in the hallway behind him, Kevin grinned with a crazy kind of pride. He held the hook pole up like an enchanted broadsword and beckoned with his free hand. "Come on, everybody! Just like in the drills; single file, no pushing or shoving." He stepped boldly into the hall. Mrs. Coffen's classroom was to the right. Kevin took a left.

Recognizing the genius of the plan, I followed him out the door. The rest of the class fell in behind as Kevin marched on, wielding the hook pole like a drum major's baton. We could hear Mrs. Coffen, still inside her classroom, issuing orders to her charges. Fire drills were her specialty. She prided herself on getting her students to their designated assembly area with choreographed precision. Last time we had drill, she openly scolded Miss Dixon for our lack of orderliness.

Knowing Mrs. Coffen would come for us as soon as she got her own class in order, we moved quietly, snaking around opening doors and slow-moving lines of younger students. By the time we reached the stairs, the hallway behind us was crowded with evacuees.

As we exited the front door of the building, Miss Dixon was there looking thoroughly perplexed. "Kevin! What is going on?"

"Fire drill. We evacuated on our own."

"What a crazy time for that!" She stepped back to let some second graders pass. "I'm very proud of you, Kevin, but you better give me the pole." She turned in a circle, as if unsure of what to do. "I suppose you might as well get on the bus. Everyone here?" She counted as we boarded, looking even more amazed that we were all there.

I took the seat closest to the front, next to Kevin, and watched as Mrs. Coffen marched her students to their designated gathering place nearby. When she had them arranged in a tight rectangle, she stepped over to our bus where our teacher was engaged in a conversation with the driver, a large man with a bushy mustache. He looked a lot like Sergeant Garcia on *Zorro* but he talked loud and non-stop, like my Uncle Charlie from Brooklyn.

Mrs. Coffen interrupted, "Miss Dixon, you need to hold off on your departure. There was some serious misconduct going on in your classroom this morning and I think it would be inappropriate to reward such behavior."

Standing on the bottom step at the open door, Miss Dixon turned slowly and broke into an open-mouthed smile. "Are you suggesting that I cancel our field trip?"

Kevin tensed visibly. My own guts seemed to solidify.

Mrs. Coffen raised her chin. "These children need to be taught a lesson."

A hook-and-ladder truck, siren winding down, pulled up behind us. A fireman in full gear jumped off and ran up to the front of the bus. He yelled past the teachers to the driver. "Hey, pal! We need you to move the vehicle. We have to get in here."

Miss Dixon grinned at her colleague and handed her the hook pole. "Be a dear and return this to my room, would you? Looks like we have to go."

The doors closed on a grim-faced woman.

Miss Dixon turned to the grinning driver. "I take it you know the way to the fair?"

He let out a booming laugh. "You kidding me? I grew up in Flushing Meadows."

I nudged Kevin as the gears ground and we got underway. "You did it, man!"

Getting no response, I looked over, expecting to find him looking straight ahead in one of his trances. Instead, he was engaged in a staring contest with Mrs. Coffen, who stood at the curb with one end of the hook pole planted on the ground, clutching her clipboard like a shield. She looked ready for battle. Kevin craned his head and she turned her body to maintain eye contact as long as possible. When the fire truck pulled in to take our place, I imagined for a moment that she might commandeer the vehicle and chase us down.

By the time we reached Newark the rain had moved on. The Manhattan skyline banished all thoughts of whatever consequences awaited us back at school. The Empire State Building and a Goodyear blimp beckoned us into The Future. I wished the bus driver would pick up the pace.

Just before we entered the Holland Tunnel, I realized my guidebook had no listing for a U.S.S.R. pavilion. My anxiety started to grow until I looked over at Kevin. He was smiling, but not in that maniacal way that signaled some impending impulsive act. For the first time since I met him, he just looked happy.

Not even Khrushchev could take that away.

About the author:

Born in 1954 in northern New Jersey, Mike moved to Georgia in 1965 and resided in the general vicinity of Atlanta. As a professional geologist, Mike has worked in the construction engineering and environmental consulting rackets since 1980. Mike wrote fiction badly for many years but with the help of an excellent editor and interesting collaborations has had recent success with 10 published short stories and numerous awards for short fiction and novellas. As a two-time finalist in The New Yorker Cartoon Caption Contest, he boasts a current total of nine words in that prestigious magazine. Mike has been married to the same Southern gal, Sally, since 1975. Together they raised two boys to adulthood and pursue a peaceful existence in an earth-sheltered home on the North Oconee River near Athens, Georgia.

CONSUMED

How some describe the aroma is a curious thing. Words like *pungent* and *stench* are typical, but one cannot so easily make sense of describing the smell of burning flesh as "sweet". As he makes his way through the cold fog and constant rain, draped in his dirty coat, he carries a bit of old food in a greasy bag tucked beneath his arm. As he stumbles along the cracked, wet pavement, a small tin of matches jangles in his pocket with every wary step. His thoughts are only briefly allowed to drift back to the good old days before the Great War. When the sun once shone through on such August days and warmed the shoulders of the busy people who walked the streets with a purpose in their step. The decimated cities now hang in bitter grey despair, their once proud skyscrapers now leaning together as if to huddle against their inevitable collapse. He recalls a time when he complained bitterly about his life, a time he would welcome back with open arms now, if he only could. Quickly, his mind races back to the business at hand. The search for his drug of choice consumes every waking moment of his wretched life.

The brutal militia that runs the city have jailed and executed most of the remaining street people, and he must keep a watchful eye out for their roving patrols. He does not fear death as much as the horror that grips his mind every day: being locked away where he can no longer fill the need that his soul demands. Knowing every crevice of the city to hide in, he makes his way toward his next fix, using the one tool he possesses that has sharpened through the years: his sense of smell. As the rain begins to turn inevitably to snow, he is even more driven to find the remedy he so desperately needs.

He turns a corner and catches a hint of the aroma he seeks. Adrenaline courses through his broken body, bringing new life to his weakened legs, and he runs as fast as he can. Flashing lights piercing through the haze confirm that his nose has not deceived him as he comes upon the scene that lifts his spirits while filling him with fear as well. The firemen move slowly to unravel the old patched hose and water slowly fills its coils as the men point the nozzle at the tenement that is now fully engulfed in flames. Muffled screams drift down to the street and are soon silenced.

Surely, he thinks, there are bodies in there. Careful not to be seen, he meanders slowly through the small gathering crowd and watches intently as the fire dies and the stretchers are brought to the entrance.

And then it happens. A black, crumbled mass that once was a human being is brought out, steaming in the cold night air, half covered by dirty rags as the militia beat away those in the crowd whose morbid fascination gets them a bit too close. He is not deterred as he focuses on the smoke still rising from the body and reaches his head over the stretcher for a chance to fill his lungs with the sweet, pungent aroma of burned human flesh. As if being transported to a new dimension, all pain is gone now as the ecstasy of the moment courses through his body and bliss replaces despair.

Too soon, his momentary relief gives way to the horror he had truly feared. He awakens on the cold, dirty floor of a prison cell, his head pounding as he feels a warm trickle of blood run down his face. The cell is dimly lit by a rusty kerosene lamp hanging on a bent nail.

Alone, he realizes the cost of his reckless drive that the satisfaction of his dreadful addiction affords him. Soon, as always, he feels his body begin to tremble, terror fills him as the need once again begins to engulf his whole body and mind. Dizzy and weak, he struggles to stand, shuffling on the dirty floor toward the bars of his cell and grasps them in his cold hands.

"Help!" he screams into the darkness. "I must get out of here now! Please!"

Staring at the lamp, his mind races madly knowing that this time he may never be free again to consume the sweet, smoky nectar he so urgently needs. He turns quickly and hears that jangle in his pocket once again. Bringing it out in the palm of his hand, the small rusty tin looks like gold in the obscure glow of the lamp. A smile slowly spills out from the side of his mouth as he opens the small container. He lights a match, and puts it to his thumb.

About the author:

Vincent Guiliano was born in raised in New Jersey and has a BA in Psychology and Creative Writing from Rutgers University; he is currently in Graduate Studies at California State University, San Bernardino and is in the process of writing an autobiographical novel. Vincent lives with his wife in Riverside, California.

WATCHER
©2014 by Amelia Perry

Kimmy huddled under the slide and stared at the far corner of the field. The corner stared back. She glanced at the deck of her house, judging the distance, and snapped her eyes back to the field. It was there—watching. She knew it with every fiber of her being. Fine hairs on the back of her neck quivered and she felt a cold sweat start to dampen her skin.

Kimmy had been playing in the new clubhouse her parents had set up at one end of the backyard. She loved it. When she climbed to the top she felt like she could see forever. Of course, it helped that the backyard overlooked a field at the bottom of a steep bank. The far side was bordered by a small river, and from the lookout she could just see the water skipping over the rocks, flashing in the sun like fairy dust.

The day was bright and beautiful, but Kimmy could sense darkness. It seemed to slink around the edge of her vision, pooling in the shadows. When she tried to look, it was gone, leaving nothing but a stain she could not focus her eyes on. She sensed its movement, so subtle she would easily convince herself when she got home that it was overactive imagination. *If* she got home.

A cloud passed over the sun and Kimmy shivered as a stale breeze chilled the sweat on her skin. Her breath came in short gasps, making it hard to hear. She tried to concentrate on breathing slower, but she was so scared. Because...because...it had moved. That was it. The cloud was just a ruse. Where? Where did it go? *It's playing with me,* she thought.

A flicker to her left made her whip her head around to find...nothing. Another trick. Kimmy turned back to the corner just in time to see the river sparkles fade, just enough, then brighten again, like a cloud's shadow passes over a plain, but faster, so much faster.

The corner. Again. She imagined she could feel the darkness reaching out for her, inviting her in. In for what? Milk and cookies? She laughed and it was a terrible, disjointed sound. She stopped, biting her tongue.

Eyes on the prize, she thought. *Maybe this is what going crazy feels like.* She stilled as her ears caught soft sounds of singing. Such a familiar song, but she couldn't place it. She started to hum along and found her lips were already moving, *"Round and round the mulberry bush, the monkey chased the weasel..."* Kimmy choked back a scream.

* * *

The corner was as far from the clubhouse as you could get and still be on the property. Farther than she could throw a ball, or a Frisbee. Farther than her big brother could shoot his bow. But it was also close. *Too* close. She knew she'd never make it to the deck and the safety (she hoped!) of the porch. It was ready for her. It wanted her to run. In a blind panic she wedged herself further underneath the slide.

Blood rushed in her ears and silent tears coursed down her cheeks. Kimmy sat in the narrow strip of shade from the slide, wedged in as tightly as she could, making herself small. She drew her knees up, wrapping her arms around them. Her throat felt tight and her face burned. Her fingers were ice cold. She took a shaky breath. She could still see the corner, she *had* to. She had to know where it was.

Kimmy heard a distant shout followed by laughter. It came from her house. Her parents were shopping and her older brother was playing video games with one of his friends. She risked a glance at the porch door. The door almost glowed: a safe place. But no one would miss her yet. Her parents wouldn't be home any time soon. She began to wonder if she'd ever see them again.

What does it want? her mind screamed. She chewed her thumb knuckle—a habit from when she was very little. At eleven and a half, she had long since left this comforting habit in the past.

The field. The corner. The deck. It was so close, the corner so *far*, and she knew. She knew she'd never make it. It was fast. Faster than thought. Faster than fear. Faster than one little blond girl with feathers in her hair.

She could definitely hit the deck with a Frisbee, she thought with a small laugh. She bit down on that laugh. Bit it and swallowed it. *What if it heard? Oh my God, what if it heard me laugh?*

Starting to lose some of her shaky grip she looked to the porch again with fevered eyes. It was so close. So close she could hit it with a rock. She should just get up and run to it. If she jumped up and just...just *exploded* into a run, as fast as she could, she would make it. She would. Kelly almost believed it. Almost.

Blood, bitter and strong, filled her mouth. Kelly looked at her hand. Her knuckle was badly cut. Could it smell the blood? Would that draw it closer, make it braver? If she just stayed and waited, would it grow bored and go away? Kelly knew that she was fooling herself. Blood was bad. *Face it girl, you're in up to your eyeballs,* she thought.

If only someone would come...her dad maybe. She knew way down inside—*knew*—that if her dad came home it would leave. It couldn't hurt her. Not if someone else was there. But she was alone. So alone.

She curled her hands into fists. The corner seemed to grow darker. The sun got lost behind a cloud and the day darkened. *It's getting stronger*, she thought, *and it's hungry. It won't wait much longer.*

More dark clouds on the horizon, pushing in from the west. The sun would soon be lost. *Now*, she thought. *Now is when it will come for me.*

She almost felt relieved. It had not been long, perhaps twenty minutes, but somehow it felt like forever. Her legs felt heavy, stiff and watery at the same time. Her hand stung where she had chewed it, but at least the blood had clotted. She was sure the blood would bring it sooner, though; she knew it in her deepest heart.

Don't look away. It will come.

She leaned her head against the bottom of the slide, staring at the corner. Nothing had moved for some time, and she knew it was a trick. Cat and Mouse. She wished with savage conviction that she was a tiger so she could scare it all the way back to the dark place it came from.

Don't look away. Don't, whatever you do.

Kimmy glanced at the sky. Dark clouds massed behind the mountains, seeking a way past, and she knew that if she was not safe in her house before that blistering mass got here, she would lose any chance of escape. Suddenly, she realized there *was* a chance. Darkness and shadow, a stripping of the light, seemed to make it faster, more mobile, *bolder*. It never moved when the sun was out; it only lurked and skulked in the dense shade of that overgrown corner. It was coming for her, make no mistake, and *soon*, but Kimmy thought she had a chance; a chance she didn't have before.

Kimmy looked around. The clouds were rapidly closing in on their little standoff, but there were still pockets of blue sky. Thunder rumbled and the air shivered with the coming storm. She got her legs under her and kept an eye on the corner. The day darkened, just a bit, and something moved.

It's coming!

Just as she got herself into a position where she could bolt from her little prison, light shot out from the clouds in molten rays, sheering the darkness and scattering the shadows. She waited just a moment, her hand in front of her like a track star. She needed to be fast like that, like a track star. Faster than thought, faster than her fear, faster than *it*, the watcher.

Silently she said goodbye to her mom and dad and her pesky big brother. In her head she kissed them all and promised she would watch over them from Heaven, if she should die today.

Then...she ran.

Time seemed to stop. Her legs were pumping and she was going nowhere. In that moment it seemed as if all her senses were in overdrive, each sound, smell, and color heightened to perfect clarity.

It was coming! Crackling grass, a breaking branch behind her. Far closer now. So close! Coming fast. *Too* fast! A silent scream welled up in her throat.

Its breath...its *breath,* a stinking reek of death and rot. The essence of nightmares! And then she was through the porch door. She wheeled, stumbled and slid on her butt. For just a second, the barest of moments, she saw something. It was dark and huge and...

Gone.

About the author:

Amelia Perry was born and raised in rural Vermont. She has been writing short stories and prose since she was a child, but has only now taken the step to get them in print. Her favorite stories are those she has written for young adults or middle grade readers. She has written in many genres, but somehow they all end up taking a dark twist, and that princess story is suddenly fraught with demons, nightmares, and bumps in the night.

Her short story "Watcher," like many of her creations, is based on a real experience that happened to her when she was about eight. The slide, the hill, and the field are all part of her family home; as was the terror she felt when she was sure something was watching her.

She gets the rest of her inspiration from her two adventurous kids, her husband's penchant for chaos, and her two crazy German Shepherd Dogs, Sampson and Shrimp Scampi.

REDEMPTION
©2014 by TJ Perkins

"Come on, baby. Just shave it off."

He lay across the bed smiling, openly displaying all of his masculinity. My eyes lingered on his chiseled nude form and I blushed slightly. Though a former Marine, his body still held remnants of perfected muscle, contoured from past years of training. His sweet and gentle nature never wavered as he waited for my response and his raw male sexuality made me yearn for his touch again, but at the moment all sexual play had stopped at the verbal request. I stood next to the bed and met his sparkling, dark eyes, still a bit stunned.

"All of it?" I looked down at myself and winced.

"All of it, baby. It'll look sooo sexy." Candle light contoured his dazzling smile as he plucked a rose from the dozen he had brought me. He touched the soft petals to my nose and trailed it slowly down my body, stopping at my hair line.

The idea of shaving myself completely twisted my guts into a knot. Sure, I willingly shaved the sides and kept it trimmed, but now the love of my life wanted it *all* gone, clean, and looking like a little girl. The very idea sparked horrid memories.

How could I tell him? How could I speak the words and relive the past, the horrible, abusive past when I was married so young and subjected to crazed torment from a man not entirely mentally stable. But that was where the memories belonged—in the past— and it was so many years ago. I almost laughed at myself as to how the past could still, without warning, give me a jolt and send my mind reeling.

"But what's wrong with it the way it is?" I still fought moving forward with the task and tried to justify it in my mind. I wanted to do it because it would make him happy. And why not? Hell, he's done anything and everything I had asked, and more, just to please me, to keep me by his side. An entire year of dinners, movies, flowers, surprise trips, and jewelry; and all he's asking is for me to remove a little bit of hair for sexual pleasure.

He reached out a hand to me and I willingly took it. "Nothing, baby." His gentle touch was soothing as he kissed my hand and gazed into my eyes. He scooted to the edge of the bed and pulled me close. "It's just that it turns me on and your body is so beautiful and perfect...well...I just think it would really look good."

He was always so wonderful and complimented me any chance he got. Unlike the last idiot I was married to, who made me feel stupid, ugly, undesirable and pathetic. No, this one was different: loving, attentive, giving, and, for lack of a better word, just a great guy.

His kiss lingered on my lips as I smiled and tried to suppress the nervousness building in my gut. My legs felt heavy as I slowly walked towards the bathroom to retrieve my razor, and bile rose in my throat as the past suddenly replayed in my mind.

"Come here, you stupid bitch!" he had screamed at me, latching onto a handful of long blonde hair as I tried to scramble away and out from under him, fighting for my life and exhausted from being choked. In his attempt to drag me back he yanked out several strands with scalp and blood attached. I screamed and cried and pleaded for him to stop, but he wouldn't and the beating continued. I flailed my arms in a desperate attempt to stop his strong hands from thrashing me across my face, forcing my head to snap from side to side, but nothing I did helped. Blood flew from my mouth as he paused and glared down at me. "How could I possibly love you?" he sneered. "Look at you, you're pathetic. So what if I screw other women! They're better than

you!"

Finally, he latched onto my upper arm, pulled me to my feet and dragged me into the bathroom of our little apartment. My heart sank as he slammed the door and pinned me against it.

"Baby? You okay?" I hadn't noticed that I had been staring at myself in the mirror, frozen in mid-movement as the past attacked my psyche. I blinked and smiled at him as his deep, sexy voice pulled me out of the depths of my memories, but they lingered and refused to stop replaying the scene in my mind as I picked up my razor and turned on the water in the sink. That's where the memories continued, back to that horrible night, just one of many.

He held the razor in his hand and turned on the water in the sink. My heart pounded uncontrollably at the very idea of what he was planning to do to me this time. His hand shot out and latched onto my neck with a vice grip. "Hold still, bitch!" He proceeded to shave me roughly, drawing blood with every stroke, manhandling me as I squirmed and tried to make him stop. "The more you move the worse it's gonna be!"

The tears wouldn't stop flowing as I clawed at his arm, hoping to make him stop, but it was a moot point. Sizzling heat and pain shot through my lower regions as he continued his grizzly escapade, smiling wickedly as I helplessly sobbed.

Within moments it was done. He stepped back and admired his handy work. The razor made a sickening clink in the sink and the water was turned off. "Look at you!" He pointed and started to laugh. I followed his gaze to my womanhood, now bald and bloody, nicks and cuts littered the tender skin from my pubic hair line to deep between my legs. "Ugly!" He placed his hands on his hips and mockingly laughed as I cried from not only the burning sensation of the cuts, but because he had yet again forced something on me that I didn't want. "You're even less than a woman now!"

Finally satisfied that he had tormented me enough for one

day, he pushed me aside and strode out of the bathroom; leaving me sobbing uncontrollably as I sat on the tiled floor amidst public hair and blood. The slamming of the apartment door was a welcomed sound.

The present settled around me and I blinked and looked at myself in the mirror, catching the reflection of my lover, best friend and soul mate anxiously waiting for me in the bedroom. A look of concern settled on his face.

"Are you sure you're alright?" he asked.

My heart jumped. I didn't want to alarm him. 'No past drama,' he had said, 'this won't work if you let past drama ruin things between us. It's not fair for me to pay for the mistakes of another.' He was right and I had done all I could over the course of our one year relationship to squash the nightmares of my past marriage and not let them interfere.

"I'm fine." I put on a brave face and started to close the bathroom door. "But I want to take care of this myself and surprise you." I gave him a wink and blew him a kiss.

"Ohhh, well, go on with your bad self, mama, but don't take too long." He smiled proudly at me as I closed the door all the way.

Alone with my reflection, I gazed at myself in the mirror and sighed. Now at the tender age of fifty my body wasn't what it used to be, though I had kept my shape even with extra weight added on from getting older. I was still attractive, but to my man I was a goddess, a queen, and he loved everything about me. He made me feel beautiful and brought out the sexuality and sensuality I thought had died so long ago.

Years ago I was made to feel less of a woman due to the fact that I was without my womanly trapping. But now the situation was different and I proudly pulled myself up and cleared my mind.

The hell with his bullshit! I thought. *I don't need a little bit of hair between my legs to make me feel like a woman. I am all woman and that man waiting for me on the other side of this door doesn't need to be convinced.*

I started to shave, gently removing the little strip of hair I had desperately held on to for most of my life. And as I shaved, the burden of the past lifted and I didn't feel so emotionally vulnerable.

With the deed completed, I smiled as I patted myself dry and made sure I didn't miss a strand before opening the door. An excited brilliant white smile and dark eyes like shining pools of onyx greeted me like a kid at Christmas. I blushed and giggled as he jumped off the bed and scooped me in his strong arms.

"Ah, baby, you actually did that for me! You just don't know how special that makes me feel." His deep kiss lingered as he gently laid me on the bed, a prelude to the love making session to come.

About the author:

TJ Perkins is a gifted and well-respected author in the mystery/suspense and fantasy genre. Her short stories for young readers have appeared in the Ohio State 6th Grade Proficiency Test Preparation Book, Kid's Highway Magazine, and Webzine'New Works Review,' just to name a few. She's placed five times in the CNW/FFWA chapter book competition. Her short story of light horror for tweens, The Midnight Watch, was published Oct 2007 by Demon Minds Magazine. Her self-publishing achievements have been greatly recognized and also TJ has conducted writing workshops for Balticon.

Finished works of her young reader's chapter books are entitled: The Fire and the Falcon (which won two chapter book awards), Wound Too Tight, Mystery of the Attic, and On Forbidden Ground. Published books in the Kim & Kelly Mystery Series include: Fantasies Are Murder, The Secret in Phantom Forest, Trade Secret, Image in the Tapestry (which won a chapter book award) and In the Grand Scheme of Things (all with GumShoe Press 2006). The Shadow Legacy series (Silver Leaf Books) book 1 has won a chapter book award.

THE FLOOD
©2014 by Kristin Swenson

It wasn't that the rains came down so much as that the water came up. Up, down, it doesn't matter, finally, when there's so much. Accounts will differ. As for the boat, believe what you will. We survived. At the time, that seemed the most important thing. A blooming miracle. Truth is, it was afterward that the real disasters came. And I'll tell you: losing my name was the least of it. "Noah's wife," my foot. Such a lovely moniker I once had. And my very own. But already I digress.

In hindsight, the flood was...well, I wouldn't exactly say "good." Clarifying, maybe. Cleansing. That's the word. Sure, a lot was lost. Lives even, and each one grieved. But for goodness' sakes, not our whole community; definitely not everybody except our immediate family. That is just not right. I mean, who wouldn't help a neighbor under such circumstances? No, the crisis brought out the best in everybody: people helping people, looking out for the creatures who couldn't swim (all those bedraggled hedgehogs), saying I love you, rediscovering the things that really matter (I can't tell you how many times I heard that phrase), realizing how little one truly needs.

Oh, it was bad all right, don't get me wrong; but wouldn't it have to be in order to be in any way good? Water like that doesn't discriminate. So for all the outward damage it did—to houses, car dealerships, government buildings, general infrastructure—it also washed away all the resentments, the petty differences that we get so twisted up about when everything else is easy. Not to say, the kids' summer camp macramé, fourth grade civics reports, my own disappointing attempts at watercolor. Gone. Without a truly cataclysmic disaster, it's hard to see, much less let go of, what weighs you down, gets under your skin, whatever you cling to. An old self, for example, locked in sepia, grinning in your one-piece at the seashore, arm around the guy who'd "be your forever" but left you after three years with two screaming kids for his bimbo of a secretary. I'm just saying.

Mostly, that's what died. The ugly stuff. As for the animals, the birds, the fish, the insects...well, the fish and the insects didn't need much help. And the others did all right. When we whittled away our own needs to the basics, there was actually plenty of space and stuff for all those other critters, too. After all, who cares about the bear on the roof when everybody's just hanging on? The leopard paddling by is a whole lot more interested in keeping its muzzle above water than in turning it on you. I could go on and on about the animals, heartbreaking and heartwarming all at once— the German shepherd dragging a mule by its prickly mane to a pile of logs that had formed a kind of raft, the eagles shuttling a warren of rabbits to higher ground. Our own floating home, where zebras felt they could share the sofa with a lynx, even offer comfort since the lynx's partner of some years had recently passed—not in the flood, before that. The cows, so apologetic about their flatulence (and it was potent, though we tried not to make faces), the ravens gathering salad fixings, the raccoons loosening tight jar lids so that the snakes might enjoy their pickled eggs. Two-legged, four-legged, feathered or finned, every body had its place and respect besides, which made the whole paradoxically self-sustaining. I could go on and on, but I won't. Just let me say: there were no dinosaurs. I mean, really. Who makes these things up?

The situation was topsy-turvy all right, and normal was just one possibility among many, but disaster? Not like what followed. I sometimes wonder these days, when I'm lost in yet another subdivision roundabout in the perennial twilight of a so-called development's ambient light, where sanity requires adopting a dull malaise and purpose is measured by one's commitment to competitive lawn-tending, if it would have been better had everything really been wiped out. Literally, the way people tell it.

Because the flood wasn't the disaster.

No, after the clouds lifted, so to speak, and the slate was wiped clean (pick your cliché), the real disasters came. You could say that calamity followed survival, and it was insidious. Tough to pin it down to one thing, in the end.

There's the booze, of course. Not that there's anything wrong with alcohol, in principle—"makes the heart glad" and all that. And once the flood had passed, you can imagine that we did some celebrating, car keys safely stowed. But you know how some people are happy drunks and some people just get mean? Noah got mean. And, man, was he drunk. Passed out cold. Something happened, that's for sure; but no one knows (or will say) exactly what set him off. Boys being boys? Who am I to judge? We gals were fine, even my daughters-in-law, and that's saying a lot.

Something happened, and Noah got his knickers all up in a twist. That's misleading because actually he was naked, and from what I gather, his birthday suit divestiture had something to do with it. Anyway, Noah cursed off our own son and his poor son after him. "Servant to his brothers," he said, for land's sakes. Give siblings about three seconds and they will have translated such a sentiment into outright slavery, laid it down like law straight from the mouth of God, and called it binding for all time. That's what our kids did, anyway, and oh the shriveling up of goodwill and just plain humanity that happened after that. You don't need me to tell you.

Surely that would have been enough to win the worse-disaster-than-a-flood golden Dingleberry Award. But there was more. I mentioned losing my name. In itself not as bad as slavery, of course, but part of something bigger and not so far from slavery, come to think of it. During the flood, folks discovered that women—even lesbians—can pray as well as priests; and "all hands on deck" really meant *all hands*. You should've seen that riveting Rosie, and with the biceps prove it. Sadly, the sentiment didn't last. I'm not sure exactly how we went from image-of-God material to dirt, but there it is and again, to far reaching effect.

Post-flood things went south for the animals, too. You see, from the very beginning, it was to be vegetarianism all around, from the most vicious be-fanged among us to the phlegmatic ruminants. Green goddess goodness was the daily *du jour, jour* in and *jour* out. Still, in the pre-flood days that I recall, everybody cheated. Yours truly was no exception. One word: bacon. (And I must say, there is nothing quite so satisfying as a lamb shank slowly braised in garlicky tomatoes, spiked with a bit of rosemary and paired with a nice burgundy, when the weather turns cold.) God knew our weakness, of course, and after the flood allowed for carnivory. Said it was okay to kill and eat just so long as we honored the lives we might take. Unfortunately, that soon devolved into trophy hunting and factory farms, hardly offset by the occasional "rub-a-dub-dub, thanks for the grub."

God told Noah that She'd never destroy the earth by flood again. Some say it'll be fire next time. As for me, fire or flood, I admit that I worry we don't much need God, that we'll destroy ourselves just fine, thank you very much. But despair's an ugly game, and there are people the world over struggling mightily to keep this great blue-green ship of ours turning with the universal tide.

These days, I see young people raising chickens, proud of how the happy fowl run about transforming garden pests into omega-3s and perfect proteins. *Local* is all the rage. Fashion-forward youth buy consignment clothes, and musicians raised on coal use bluegrass to protest mountain-top removal. Noah wants to downsize and talks about swapping our energy-eating A.C. for a wrap-around porch. My son's family lives where he can walk to work and the kids to school (where the girls have the same homework and soccer practice as their brothers). They even tore up what little lawn they had and planted native species fed by compost. There's birth control, rape is prosecuted as a violent crime, and most places have curb-side recycling. People of repute, even Senators, aren't above reproach. Nations favor conversation over bombs, and I've found that arugula grows nearly year-round in our back yard.

When I take all these things into account, it occurs to me that maybe disaster (or not) is in the telling—how we do and of what should follow. After all, when everything else has washed away, blown away, burned away, what are we left with? Words. As it was in the beginning, even now. Out of the rubble, the ashes, the dust of the earth, it is words—the right words—that just may save us in the end.

About the author:

Kristin Swenson is the author of Bible Babel: Making Sense of the Most Talked About Book of All Time (Harper Perennial, 2011, and now available in both Portugese and Korean) as well as two other books and provided creative translations with commentary for The Voice Bible. In addition to academic articles and news outlets, Kristin has written for The Christian Century, Beliefnet., CNN.com, The Washington Post's On Faith, Good Morning America's online religion page. She regularly contributes to The Huffington Post and Publishers Weekly. With a Ph.D. in the history and literature of ancient Israel, Kristin earned tenure in Religious Studies at Virginia Commonwealth University in Richmond, VA. Following a fellowship at the Virginia Foundation for the Humanities, she resigned from VCU and moved to Charlottesville, where she is affiliated with the University of Virginia. In addition to speaking engagements, her work includes historical fiction and playwriting as well as nonfiction.

You can find her at www.kristinswenson.com.

CAPISCE?

"So, whaddya think of coming over to my mom's for dinner?" As with most of his propositions, Joey put it out there more as a hypothesis than an invitation. A breakthrough, nonetheless. For four years, Joey intrigued me with tales of his family's antics at Sunday dinner: he Italian-born aunts and uncles with their old country stories, his slutty sister's perpetual love crises, his long-dead daddy's strict rules still enforced by his sainted mama.

Joey spoke of his mother's specialties—lasagna, bragiole, gnocchi, and dishes I had never heard of—as if they were sacraments. Brought up on the meat-and-potatoes diet of the American farm culture, I could go for something new, especially if it led to what I really hungered for: a proposal.

"Sounds okay. Maybe I can get Jonathan down here." My six-year-old son stayed with my folks upstate while I worked on the Verrazano Narrows Bridge. I had a good job with an environmental company, monitoring lead dust as they removed the old paint. It paid well and I needed the money. For the duration of the project, I lived in a crappy Brooklyn apartment.

Joey winced at the sound of my little boy's name. "Whoa! Let's save that for another time. Let my mom get used to you first." He put an arm around me. "For the time being, she don't need to know about Jonathan. She's a little old fashioned."

"Yeah, I know. Good Catholic woman. Raised in the shadow of the Vatican. I got it." Having a child has never been exactly conducive to dating but Joey treated Jonathan as if he were his own. He even bothered to take us places far from Staten Island: Jones Beach, the Bronx Zoo, even Atlantic City.

It could wait.

* * *

Mama Trapani came to New York about the time Mussolini got whacked in Mezzegra. Fifty years later, she might as well have just stepped off the boat from Sicily. At first meeting, she showed me a grainy photo of a young woman at the docks surrounded by American GIs. Her hair remained just as black but her face and frame had filled out as if she were stockpiling against the return of the Fascists and re-imposition of wartime rationing.

The little English she spoke came only out of absolute necessity. She made up for it with a vast vocabulary of facial expressions. The third time I walked into her house, her eyes went from me to Joey in a way that clearly said, 'Can't you find a nice Italian girl?' She may have feared having grandchildren contaminated by genes that favored pale, freckled skin and straight, straw-blonde hair. Like it really mattered to me. More children did not figure in my future plans.

Not the best-looking guy I ever dated, Joey had strong hands and the build of a wrestler. His broad face bore signs of some hard times; a few pockmarks, a linear scar that ran from eye to ear on one cheek and a nose just a little bit misaligned. He looked tough and I liked the idea of having him there in case my annoying and occasionally violent ex-husband started coming around again. Always gentle with my boy and I, Joey had a sweet smile that washed the faults away.

The kitchen atmosphere felt saturated with aromas that clung to the skin with what I imagined were airborne droplets of fat. Joey kissed his mama's forehead. She rewarded him with sharp words accompanied by menacing gesticulations with a wooden spoon. She avoided looking at me and went back to showing Veronica, the kid brother's dark-haired fiancée, the secrets of preparing Chicken Parmigiana.

The women spoke Italian as we passed and shared a laugh that just seemed at my expense. I only picked up a single word but I held my tongue until we got to the living room. "So, Joey! What's a *'donnina'?*"

Joey grimaced and tipped his head side to side. "Ma thinks you're too pretty to be a good girl. Watch out. She may try to fatten you up."

Not much of a definition but I got the idea. "If you mean for making grandchildren, forget about it. She doesn't want any that look like me."

If Joey had any words of comfort to share, he let the opportunity pass. I settled into one of his grandmother's ancient armchairs while he made the rounds with his aged relatives. Based on past experience, I would have at least half an hour to wait and soak up the ambience.

The décor contained a strange mix of Old World elegance and New World cheesiness. On the one hand, the ecru lace tablecloth, the antique china, the matching Burl Wood cabinet and credenza. On the other, the wallpaper embossed with velvet filigree, overstuffed furniture with clear plastic covers. Gaudy chandeliers in every room cast it all in a soft Parmesan glow.

One theme dominated it all: the Blessed Virgin Mary. Mama Trapani honored Her in much the same way that an Elvis freak paid tribute to the King of Rock and Roll. Plaster statuettes, gilt-framed prints, and even a tapestry showed pretty much the same view of the long-suffering Holy Mother of Jesus.

Ten years dead, Papa Frank remained a presence. A large black and white photograph of the old man stared out from the mantelpiece. He looked like a real son of a bitch and I sensed no approval from him. Mama Trapani would still look up and cross herself whenever she entered the room. I did my best to avoid his judgmental gaze.

Joey returned with a trio of older men, better dressed than his usual friends did and a little more serious. They traded a few off-color jokes but nothing really dirty. A couple of them flirted with me and Joey's twenty-year-old sister Denise. She may have matched her mother's dark-haired ideal of Italian womanhood but she tended to push her assets with too little fabric and too much makeup. These men seemed to know where to draw the line. No touching. No dirty words. They had class. After twenty minutes or so, the oldest man looked at his watch. The joking stopped and the men exchanged glances that suggested some urgent purpose.

Joey locked his gaze on Denise. I saw her nod once before she stood and tapped my shoulder. "Let's go watch some TV."

Not quite my confidante, Denise still helped me negotiate the mysterious household protocols. Sometimes amused at what she termed my "country girl" ways, she took it upon herself to educate me in the finer points of urban fashion and behavior. Hopefully, I could count on her for the secrets of her mother's cooking since Mama Trapani obviously did not regard me as daughter-in-law material. For the moment, I wanted to hear more, maybe learn a little about what Joey did for a living.

Denise nudged me a little harder than appropriate. Having no interest in television I pretended to not notice. She put her face directly in front of mine "We gotta go. They gotta talk business."

"I'd love to hear it. I'm interested in what—"

Denise grabbed my wrist and pulled. "We go now." She led me upstairs to her room, turned on the TV, and lit up a joint as she sank back into the pillows and oversized plush toys at the head of her bed. I took a seat on an ottoman next to her. We did not speak for a good ten minutes as a soccer match played out on a massive old console that might have pre-dated Disco. Her lack of response at every goal said that Denise did not give a rat's ass about the game.

I broke the silence. "So, Denise, the other night, I'm at Joey's apartment and he comes home with his shirt spattered with blood and a baseball bat to match. He been in a fight or something?"

She stared at the screen until the game went to commercial. "Probably found a pick-up game. They can get a little out of hand."

"That's kinda what he said, but after he showers I find him out burning the bat and his clothes in the backyard grill. Tells me the bat's no good. Made him foul out."

"Sounds like the Joey I know."

Denise was not being straight with me. I wanted to share the horror I felt that night and Joey's strange behavior. The way he squeezed the metal can of charcoal lighter until it sputtered like a robot with diarrhea, cursed it for being empty and threw it at the cat. Hard. He loved that cat. As the flames consumed the cloth and wood, he looked possessed, not the sweet guy I thought I knew.

I pulled a newspaper clipping from my purse. "I came across this a couple of days ago."

Denise lit up a cigarette and read the story of a heroin dealer's body found in the trunk of a car down at Rockaway Beach. She tilted her head from side to side, dark curls bouncing, as if the words were just the notes of a familiar tune. "Oh, yeah, Vinny Varese. He raped my cousin. He won't be missed by many."

"Is that what it was about?"

"They're all fucking rapists, these guys. I'm sure it was just business. The thing with my cousin is just a bonus."

"Was Joey involved?"

Denise sat up straight on her bed and pivoted to face me. "Look, there are things you don't ask around here. Don't ask me. Don't ask my brother. Don't ask nobody." She grabbed my elbow and applied pressure at the joint, making it hurt. "For God's sake, just shut the fuck up about it. *Capisce*?"

I had become accustomed to the cursing. Out of Mama Trapani's house, with Joey's family and friends, obscenities were just about as constant as cicadas in August. A default. One night at my apartment, I hear this outburst from the bathroom as if Joey's caught his dick in a metal zipper. Turns out he dropped his comb in the toilet. My dad lost half a finger to a fan belt on his tractor and never made half the noise.

Besides the grossly exaggerated body language, I noticed the way Joey's associates deliberately abused the rules of the English language. They all knew better. Their parents sent them to Parochial schools where embittered nuns with rock maple rulers hammered home conjugations and verb-subject agreement with the same zeal as the Ten Commandments and Stations of the Cross. Cursing and bad grammar signaled serious business and bad behavior.

Denise did not wait for my answer, not that I had one. The sound of chairs dragging across the floor signaled dinner. I silently followed her downstairs to the dining room, wondering what realm I had entered.

Evidently, nine people did not constitute a big family gathering at this house. The massive table could accommodate at least three more. My mother would have been frantic dealing with such a group. Mama Trapani looked serene as she took her seat by the empty chair at the head of the table, that place set for an invisible presence.

A frail man across the table winked at me. Denise warned me about her uncle Alfredo. He sported a spare but neatly trimmed mustache and the pale gray skeleton of a pompadour that spoke of a once-handsome and important man. He smiled at me as if I were the first woman he had seen after a long stay in prison. "I like blondes. I was married to one for forty-five years."

Denise pushed his wheelchair in until his protruding gut touched the table. "Uncle Alfredo, you were married to Aunt Cecilia for forty-eight years."

"Yeah, but she lost her hair after forty-five." He slapped the table and gave a wheezing laugh that sounded as if it might be his last.

Denise sat down next to me and whispered, "She was getting chemo at the time. He tells that joke every year."

Veronica took note of my horror. "He doesn't get out from the home much. It's his birthday."

Mama Trapani glared and shook her fork. "*Alfredo! Hanno rispetto.*"

The old man shrugged and busied himself with the pasta. He clearly did not wish to challenge the old woman's gaze.

Denise explained *sotto voce,* "Cecilia was her big sister. Another glass of wine and he'll start bawling about her."

Mama Trapani looked up to see if I was joining in the group mumble as Alfredo said some kind of Grace. I followed Denise's lead, doing my best to look like a good Catholic, fingertips pressed together, eyes cast down. It would still take a bottle of black hair dye, a deep tan, and a bucket of ass widener to make me fit her mama's image of a proper Italian girl.

Joey held the salad for me to serve myself. "Make sure you get some croutons before Alfredo gets to them." When the kitchen phone rang, Joey's smile vanished. He snatched the tongs from my grasp and passed the bowl to Denise. "I'll get it, Ma. Business, you know."

As he hurried to the kitchen, I looked to Denise. She shrugged and served herself a tomato wedge. "Only freaking phone we got in the house. Papa Frank's rule. Sheesh."

Mama Trapani muttered something that sounded like a prayer, looked at the ceiling and then glared at Denise.

I strained to follow the kitchen conversation. If the cops were coming for Joey, I stood ready to leave the country with him. He would change once out of his mother's orbit. Away from this psychotic family, he would not have to do their dirty work, whatever it might be.

Denise nudged me. "So, you gonna go see your folks over the holidays? You going upstate? When are you going?"

Odd for her to fire questions at me that way. She seemed to be providing noise to cover Joey's conversation, which made me determined to hear it. I kept my answers short. "Yes. Yes. The twenty-second."

Joey said a word he had used on me a few times. "*Bambolina!*" It sounded so sweet that I never questioned the meaning. I started to respond but realized he was still on the phone.

He smacked the receiver down, turned in a circle, then dialed. He worked his temples as he waited for an answer. "Put Francesca back on. I know. I know. Oh, yeah, *come si chiama?* Still here. Not for long."

There was another term he used around me, but not directly.

Whenever he saw me look up, he would wink and smile; another pet name, or so I thought. I started to wonder.

"*Cara mia!* January, June. Whatever makes you happy."

Denise poked me and was about to speak when I cut her off. "Who the hell is Francesca?"

The clatter of silver on porcelain ceased. All eyes turned to Mama Trapani. She shrugged and shoveled a forkful of chicken into her mouth. Veronica answered as if on the old woman's behalf, "Joey's fiancé. Didn't he tell you?"

Joey, still in the kitchen, apparently oblivious, went on. "*Come si chiama,* she's history."

I turned to Denise. "What's that mean? The *come si chiama* or whatever?"

Back when I started dating Joey, she invited me to a 'girls' night out'. New to the city, I showed up at the appointed time in a frilly party dress. Denise answered the door wearing a black leather mini-skirt. She gave me the same "*Are you kidding me?*" look she had that night. "You didn't know? I thought you were just being a good sport."

Veronica was more than happy to fill me in as she snagged the last dinner roll. "In this case, it roughly translates as 'what's her name?'"

It might as well have translated to 'practice pussy'. The son of a bitch! Joey suddenly noticed my stare. There went the wink. Had I been holding an ice pick, I would have made it permanent.

Mama Trapani locked her gaze on me and spoke with a tremor. "You been with my son two whole years and you learn nothing of our language? What makes you think you good enough for him?"

It had actually been four years I had been with Joey. Four fucking years of secretive dating and elaborate excuses. I suddenly understood why we went everywhere but Lower Manhattan and Staten Island. Why everything he owned bore a Yankees logo but we always went to see the Mets. He did not want to be seen with me close to home or anywhere he frequented with his main squeeze.

When Joey took his seat next to me, the initial shock gave way to a roiling mix of anger, horror, and hate. Perhaps the grin set me off, but without pausing to think, I stood and elevated a fine specimen of Grandma Trapani's old world china. I brought it down hard, parmigiana and all, on the top of his skull. *"Bastardo!"* Not much of a venture into bilingualism, but the best I could do at the moment. Maybe something I heard in a movie, a lousy cognate an American third grader could have interpreted.

Uncle Alfredo nodded as I squeezed by. He liked a good show. As I descended the front stoop, the old woman shrieked. I fantasized a chicken bone lodged in her throat.

* * *

Three months passed before I heard from Joey. As the phone rang, I stared at the number on the caller ID and considered my options. My rational self wanted just to count the number of rings to gauge his desperation. My vengeful self wanted to tell him to fuck off. My lonely self just picked up.

"Hey! Just wanted to know how ya doin'." The old familiar voice had some new seasoning; a blend of concern and contrition.

"Don't even start, Joey. I got nothing to say to you, but I'll give you thirty seconds."

"Look, I know I didn't exactly do right by you. I want to make it up."

"What about Francesca? You dumped her?"

A long silence ensued. I could picture him biting his lip, thinking up a lie. I actually missed that look.

"Let's just say things ain't working out like we thought they would."

"So she dumped you?"

"Whoa! What's it matter who's dumping who? It's not important."

"What's important, Joey, is that I'm not coming back to a three-way relationship. I want ex-clu-si-vi-ty. You can't live with that, don't call." I hung up.

The phone rang not five minutes later. "*Bellissima!* What do I gotta do to get you back?"

Having had plenty of time to think things over, I spelled out my terms in short order. To my amazement, he accepted. His timing was good. My Verrazano Bridge project had finished but it would be two weeks before I got my last paycheck and a month for my bonus. A new job in Michigan was coming up but I did not want to put Jonathan through another move. He had friends and family in New York. Life with Joey took on new appeal.

* * *

We went to a grungy little bar not two blocks from Mama Trapani's. My kind of joint. Cozy. Quaint. Definitely not a franchise. Brick walls painted nearly smooth. "This would have made a good place to get adjusted before dinner at your mother's."

Joey cringed and led me to a booth way in the back. "Sit tight. Frannie should be here in a minute." Then he left.

I sipped on the house wine and fended off half a dozen Guidos before spotting Joey and some girl at the door. They carried on a five-minute conversation with their hands before entering. She looked a lot like I imagined, jet-black hair done up like a punk rocker, Ferrari-red lipstick and nails to match. She had the high cheekbones and full sensuous face that I could picture expanding into a likeness of Joey's mother before she was thirty. From where I sat, she looked like a total whore.

They took their time making it back my way. Guys at the bar greeted Francesca and she made a point of exchanging words with each of them. I got it. This was *their* bar. This was *her* turf.

Francesca may have thought me hard of hearing or else had no shame about being a bitch. Ten feet away, she tilted her head in my direction and spoke to Joey. "So that her? She looks like a total whore!" Her accent was pure Brooklyn. I could have hated her just for that.

Joey rolled his eyes and presented her. "This is Francesca. Why don't you two get acquainted while I get some drinks?" He stepped over to the bar before I could either protest or even tell him what I wanted.

Francesca slid into a chair across from me and started right in. "That the house wine you're drinking? It's swill. Try the Chianti; much better for the complexion."

"I'm fine." I finished the wine and tried to get Joey's attention.

Francesca let me know she had the owner's manual. "He ain't gonna look over here. He's gotta talk to his jerk friends." She shrugged. "So, he tells me he took you over to his mother's. Think you could handle a lifetime of dinners at Mama Trapani's? That creepy Uncle Alfredo? That bitch Veronica?"

"Mama Trapani and Alfredo will probably die off pretty soon. I can always kill Veronica."

"Good answer." Francesca smiled briefly. "Heard you busted a piece of Grandma Trapani's fine china. You're lucky to be alive."

"Guess it comes out of Joey's inheritance." I did not know how much longer I could maintain my front. My own words sounded almost foreign. I hated to think I was turning into one of these people.

Joey came back with a bottle of wine and three glasses. He set it all on the table and slid in next to me. "They got that Chardonnay stuff you like."

Francesca's dark eyes flared. She had picked up her purse from the bench seat and put it in her lap when she saw Joey approach. When she noticed that I was looking at it, she fumbled inside as if trying to find some reason for having moved it. She pulled out and applied more lipstick to a mouth that already looked like it might have come with a rubber-ball nose and oversized shoes.

Joey served me first. When he went to serve Francesca, she pushed the bottle away and looked on with disgust as Joey and I clinked our glasses. She got right to business. "So, what's it gonna be, Joey? Me or her. I want you to say right now, in front of her."

Joey pushed out his lower lip like a slug and fanned out his thick fingers. You would have thought he had not yet made up his mind. Without a word, he dipped his head in my direction, sipped his wine, and took a sudden interest in the many bottles behind the bar.

Francesca started spewing words as if trying to get all of her thoughts out before she was too choked up to talk. "How can you do this to me? You piece of shit!" She broke down, but only for a minute. When Joey put his hand on her wrist, she recoiled. Her voice came back low and husky. "Don't touch me, you fucking bastard!"

As she slid out of the booth, Joey got up and stood oddly at the end of the table. I imagined he did not want Fran to have a clear shot at his crotch.

"You got a lot of enemies, Joey! I now consider them my friends. Just hope we don't meet up again."

He glanced at her left hand. Fran glared back and pulled at the ring. She looked at me, tears running freely down her full, heavily rouged cheeks. "Ya got any lotion? I'm retaining a little water and this piece of shit wants his fucking ring back."

I pulled a small plastic bottle from my purse and looked away. My guess was she was actually retaining Mama Trapani's cream sauce as the old woman prepped her for childbearing.

Fran held the container up to the light. Her tears did not at all dilute her bitchiness. "Oh my God! You put this stuff on your body? No wonder you're flaking like a lizard." After a minute, she seized my ring finger and slid the symbol of Joey's love on my hand. It turned stone down, at least a couple of sizes too big, which seemed to piss her off even more. "Hope it brings you as much fucking happiness as it did me."

A circle of quiet enveloped us. Several minutes passed before the noise level recovered. Joey took a seat opposite me. Pursing his lips, he regarded my hand. "I can get that resized. I got a guy."

I pulled the ring off and flicked it across the table like a paper football. "I don't really care much for diamonds."

"The hell you saying? It's two fucking carats! It appraised at eight grand!" Joey took my left wrist as if he were strangling a snake, stared into my eyes, and slipped the ring back on the appropriate finger. "This was my mother's engagement ring. I want you to fucking marry me; become part of my family."

I held my fingers together and tipped the stone to catch the feeble bar light. It was a gorgeous piece of rock. "I don't want your mama's ring. I don't want Francesca's ring. I want a big fat ruby."

Francesca would have enjoyed the pain in Joey's eyes. "Okay! That's what you want, that's what you'll get." He reached out with his palm up.

I gave in to a sudden urge to massage my knuckles. "In the meantime, I'll keep this as a token of your devotion."

He closed his eyes and pressed his right fist against his sternum with his left hand. I couldn't tell if he was praying, suffering chest pain, or physically restraining himself from slugging me. He inhaled and exhaled loudly and grabbed the edges of the table as if he was either going to flip it over or cling to it until he had his composure back. It was a good minute before he spoke. "All right, but for God's sake, take good care of that ring. Oh, and yourself, of course."

We made a date for dinner at Mama Trapani's. Joey swore to announce our engagement there and then.

* * *

I had already packed most of my stuff in anticipation of moving back to my parents' place upstate. My crummy basement apartment came furnished so all I had to take was my clothes, a few books, and some photographs. My favorite shot was the one on top of the east tower of the Verrazano Bridge. I had to pull some strings to get Joey up there but he wanted to impress his friends.

I could remember the moment as if it had just happened. Joey handed my co-worker Spiros my cheesy little Instamatic and took two steps back. If he had taken four, we would have been side by side. Instead, there's Joey, front and center with me in the background, kind of lumped in with the city skyline and distant clouds. I could hear his voice, pushy and loud. "Take the fuckin' picture! I'm freezing my ass off here!"

Spiros obeyed. It was the last shot on the roll. No retakes, no second chances.

I hated Joey's smug look. He had gotten what he was after. There I stood, nameless, alone, part of the scenery. Then it hit me. When we met at the bar, he had not introduced me to Francesca. Even when he chose me over her, it was with a nod and a look, no declaration of love eternal.

My answering machine had a message from my sister, Pam, down in Georgia. She had a way of saying my name, my whole name, as if it were a sentence. I relished hearing her voice, still pure upstate. "So, anyway, they're looking for a nature interpreter at this State park where I'm working. I figure with your environmental background you'd be perfect. The pay's not good but living's cheap here. I'm renting a house and have room for you. We'll get paid to hike in the woods, teach kids about nature, breathe fresh air. Just like we talked about when we were going to school. Jonathan will love it down here. Give me a call."

The plan crystallized immediately. I knew of a pawnshop over in Jersey, not far from the train station. I sold my high school ring there one desperate week for fifty bucks. I could get at least a couple of grand for Mama Trapani's ring. I would have my cousin mail Joey the claim ticket from San Francisco. He would never come after me that far from New York. Besides, he could look there all he wanted. I was heading south.

I snatched the five-by-seven from the dresser. My hands shook so much I could not get the photo out. I smacked the frame on a bedpost and peeled away the shards of glass. The right side of the picture suffered damage but that did not bother me. I ripped it down the middle, taking all of Joey but his elbow out of the scene. I slid the half with Manhattan and me into a book and dropped the remainder into an empty, rusted trashcan. Joey's image curled like a worm on hot pavement. I leaned in so close my voice echoed off the sides, in pure, undiluted English.

"By the way, it's Elizabeth, you rat bastard!"

About the authors:

SUSAN ZIMMERMAN: Born in rural New Jersey in 1967, Susan enjoyed a pleasant childhood around the Adirondacks of Upstate New York. Married to Mr. Wrong at 21 until getting knocked around lost its charm, she started a new life as a single mom of a baby boy in NYC in 1993. Found work refurbishing the Verrazano Narrows Bridge while pursuing an overlong relationship that turned out to be empty promises. Susan and son headed to Georgia in 1997 and finally got it right. Susan acquired an education that prepared her for a career in the environmental sciences, engineering and commercial construction. Having learned how to deal with men the hard way, Susan now shares her experiences through writing, She currently enjoys life with her husband Charlie (Mr. Right) in the Appalachian foothills of Georgia.

MIKE TUOHY: Born in 1954 in northern New Jersey, Mike moved to Georgia in 1965 and resided in the general vicinity of Atlanta. As a professional geologist, Mike has worked in the construction engineering and environmental consulting rackets since 1980. Mike wrote fiction badly for many years but with the help of an excellent editor and interesting collaborations has had recent success with 10 published short stories and numerous awards for short fiction and novellas. As a two-time finalist in The New Yorker Cartoon Caption Contest, he boasts a current total of nine words in that prestigious magazine. Mike has been married to the same Southern gal, Sally, since 1975. Together they raised two boys to adulthood and pursue a peaceful existence in an earth-sheltered home on the North Oconee River near Athens, Georgia.

ALL OF ME
©2014 by Catharine Leggett

She's left it too long. Lily doesn't know why she leaves things until the last minute. She's given up on the idea she'll ever change. It isn't all her fault. Every time she thinks to go shopping for a dress, something gets in the way. The car called it quits; one of the kids needed the money she was going to spend, all the comings and goings at the house, the help she's giving Sheila with the wedding, and at her age, with her health issues, well, she only has so much energy. But never mind all that. She's here now, and Brittany, a cute little thing—oh she wishes Ben could meet her, what a fine match they would be—is doing her best to give great service.

"I'll keep bringing you all the dresses that look right for a wedding and you can try them on, even if it's something you think you'd never wear. Why not? Now that you're here. You might just surprise yourself, you know. You don't know until you try." Brittany had a plan of action when she heard Lily's request for a dress to wear to a friend's wedding, got right to the task when Lily told her she was in a bit of a rush, as usual.

So sincere, so attentive, how could she say no to trying on everything? And just like her kids, Brittany had a little touch of she-knows-what's-best. They all know what's best when they're twenty-something.

Lily won't let Brittany into the fitting room. She is wearing her best underwear, but Brittany might be shocked by the safety pin she uses to hold her panties up, though the lace is still pretty. It's just the elastic in the waistband's shot. Like her: stretched thin, exasperated. Her bra, well, it's her only comfortable one, and the only one that will take care of *the girls,* and the elastic at the back is so frayed it looks like a wire-haired terrier with a fur condition. She won't be buying a new one any time soon. A double-G cup costs the earth, never mind where do you even find one?

Lily examines the layers of dresses hanging from the hooks. She'll start with the red one.

"Everything fitting okay?" Brittany calls from outside the change room.

"Just fine." Lily wonders how she'll manage to squeeze into it; it has such a short zipper.

"No problems?"

"No problems."

Her wedding dress was red, a polyester fabric that crumpled up into nothing, with a rhinestone pin at the base of her cleavage. Diamonds to her. With her dark hair, the large fake pin, her shapely shape, Nick called her *my Liz.*

They got married at Christmas, another reason for the red dress. Nick bought a new suit; new to him. He bought it at the Sally Ann. They thought they were the bee's knees, the cat's pajamas, the two of them, in their wedding clothes that cost all of fifty dollars. Makes her laugh thinking about it. He in his too large old-man-piss pants suit—at least wool was appropriate for the time of year—and she in her Kmart dress, all of twenty-four dollars, and even then she thought it too expensive. And after the ten minute ceremony witnessed by two clerks, total strangers, they went for surf and turf at the Steer and Stein, and got a booth at the back in the corner. To celebrate the news of their marriage, the waitress took flowers from another table and plunked them into their vase, then went to talk to the man playing piano. After they finished their dinners, while still wearing their lobster bibs, the piano player announced their special occasion to a few other diners and insisted they dance. The only two on the dance floor, the disco ball sparkling overhead. He had a special song for them. What's the name of the song? It's going to drive her nuts; it's on the tip of her tongue. Oh she hates that when she can't remember, and it was one of her favorites, too. Never mind, it'll come, eventually.

They danced the rest of the evening. Happy. In love.

Lily unzips the red dress, hoists it above her head, feels the ache in her arms and shoulders as she tries to wriggle into it.

Nick, tall, thick chested, lots of hair, big rough hands from working outside, a man's man, a glint of playfulness in his eyes, and such a capacity for fun in those days. He'd up and do anything on the spur of the moment and Lily willing to go right along with him. He got them on a logging truck that took them into the interior of B.C. where they ended up living for six months on a hippie commune. Living off the land, they called it then. The land and the odd welfare cheque. They thought they lived for free. She knows better now. Nothing comes for free. Or the fishing boat, when he found temporary jobs during a herring run. She's never been sicker in her life. High swells, and though she didn't know it yet, the swell in her belly—still too early to know it was two. *Spontaneous* defines Nick to this very day.

The red dress won't do. Too clingy. Now *there's* a laugh. Clingy? She can't get it past her boobs. It might have fit a number of sizes ago. "I think I'm going to need a bigger size," she calls to Brittany. She honestly thought she was a sixteen, but realizes probably an eighteen. Maybe bigger?

"I've got something in a blue floral," Brittany calls from the other side of the door. "I think it would be lovely with your coloring. It's a cute dress. "

Her coloring? What would that be? Tired blue, verging on grey? She's no beauty, not anymore. She's three times the person she was when she and Nick hooked up. Anyway, she isn't one for florals. They could either be too matronly or too girly. When was the last time she wore anything that was cute?

"Okay, I'll give it a try." Brittany's doing her best. It's late on a

Saturday afternoon, and she must have sore feet by now, this place being as busy as it is. She's so sincere and trying so hard; Lily will go along with her suggestions.

The blue floral sails over the top of the dressing room door. "There you go."

Ben looked a little blue this morning. He came in early, on his way to work, traipsing down the hall in his heavy boots so it woke her up. He could only manage to get part of the day off.

She shouted from her bed upstairs. "Take off those boots. I just did the floors yesterday."

"I've got a Tim's for you. What the hell, I can't even do you a favor without you giving me shit?"

She looked at her watch. 6:45. So much for sleeping in. She heard Thunder on the stairs. Next thing she knew, Thunder was straddling her, running his big sloppy tongue over her face. She turned her head from side to side to avoid the lashing, but it was no use. Finally she rubbed him behind the ears and gave in to the licking. "You big clumsy goof of a mutt."

Ben stood in the doorway smiling, holding two large double-doubles. His face looked like it had been put through a meat grinder, all scratched and bruised and puffy.

"What happened to you?"

"Someone jumped me on the way home from the bar last night."

"How drunk were you?"

"Not at all. He jumped me from behind."

"Did you say something to provoke him?"

"What the hell. Why do you always think it's my fault?"

"You need stitches."

"I'm okay. I washed the cut and put Polysporin on it."

"I can just imagine how this will look in Allison's wedding pictures." Just once, wouldn't it be nice to wake up with nothing but a normal day ahead? Without some kind of catastrophe? Sheila, the mother of the bride, will kill him, never mind how Allison will feel. The groom won't care, he's so much like Ben.

"You've got to learn to control your temper and walk away from these things."

"I haven't got time for your lecture," Ben said. "I'm out of here. I'm leaving Thunder for the day."

She shouted at him, "Get back here! I've got too much to do to take care of the dog. And I need your cell phone in case Sheila has to get in touch with me. I'm still helping her with the wedding."

He tossed his cell phone on the bed. "Don't lose it."

The red dress lies on the floor. She'll hang it up later, once she's tried on a few more dresses. Sure she will, just like the way she cleaned her room yesterday. Sweet, dear Lindsay helped as much as she could. "Mom, have you ever hung up anything in your life?" Lindsay's so efficient, way more efficient than Lily; she has no idea where she inherited the tidy gene. "Mom, you need to concentrate on one thing at a time." Lindsay sounded like the parent. "You're too easily distracted."

She had every intention of cleaning her room, but then the phone rang, and Mabel needed someone to go to a doctor's appointment with her, to hear the results of her biopsy, and that meant a bus ride across town. Mabel couldn't go alone; that's no way to treat a friend. After, they stopped for a chocolate sundae at We've Got the Scoop, to take some of the sour away with a bit of sweet. The rest of the day she spent with Sheila helping her decorate the reception hall. In her room sat the piles of clothes, layer upon layer, settling like sediment, measuring off the phases of her life. And the other piles, mostly the stuff she got at garage sales—jewelry, shoes, purses, all waiting to be sorted. She's disgraceful; she knows it.

"You still good?" Brittany calls.

"It's going to take me at least a half hour to get through all these, deary," Lily answers. She's already in a sweat and she has many more to go.

Tiffany's bridesmaids were wearing blue, so she should avoid that color, though no one would confuse her for one of them, that's for sure, since she's about forty years older and she wishes she was only forty pounds heavier. It's true, any bit of stress and she heads for the fridge, seeking comfort, can't seem to make herself stop. A person needs treats when stress whooshes through her house every single day like a tornado. If she could go to a spa where people in white coats and soothing voices commit themselves to her care, knead her knotted muscles, offer sympathy for all she has to contend with, prepare healthy meals for her every day, give her positive reinforcement to make her feel good about herself, she could stop eating. She'd become slim.

What will Thunder have done to her house? He's better than he was, but if he's left too long he starts chewing. He ate two legs off the coffee table as easily as if they were pretzels, and now she uses bricks to hold it up. A few days later, he ate the living room curtains—just the bottoms. They still provide privacy and keep the light out on days she doesn't want anything to do with the outside world, when it's all she can do to get out of bed, lie on the couch and watch TV, when all she wants is to be left alone. And then there's the pooping.

She shouldn't stay too late tonight at the wedding, though she promised Sheila she'd help with the buffet, and that meant the clean up after. Anything to help her friend save money. Sheila has about as much of it as she has—next to nothing. But it should be a nice wedding. The reception room looked lovely, even romantic, with white streamers and paper wedding bells, bows on all the chairs.

"The blue dress makes me look old," Lily calls to Brittany.

"Well, we definitely can't have that."

"I *am* old. Not much I can do about it."

"No you are not," Brittany's voice scolds. "You're only as old as you feel."

"Oh, if you only knew. Just you wait, Brittany, some day you may understand. Hopefully not." Today she aches in every joint. She wishes she could afford the medication to ease the inflammation.

She looks at the yellow, black and white striped dress and

thinks why not just wear a yield sign? Everyone would see her coming. She should try it on so she can report to Brittany. At least she can wriggle into it easily enough. It slides down easily over her hips; she turns to the mirror. It's way too big, and she can't really find words to describe it. A giant lemon? Oversized canary? No, Big Bird, that's who she is. She looks at the tag. She's forgot her glasses; is she reading that right? Size 24! Is that how Brittany sees her? That big? She's made a mistake, grabbed the wrong size. It accents her hair, but that's all she can say about it. She can't hold back her laughter.

What if Nick saw her in this? What would he say? Or any of her kids? Peter, for instance, he'd have something smart to say, the connoisseur-of-everything that he is. She can imagine the insults.

Peter phoned last night. She was so out of it. "Hi, Mom, how are you? Did I wake you? I hope not."

"What do you expect? It's three am. How much money do you want?"

"Hey, I never asked for money, did I? What if I was just phoning to say hi from England? Can't a son do that?"

"Yes, a son can and *you* never would. How much? I'm down to my last pennies, just so you know."

"Just a couple hundred, Mom. Can you wire it in the morning?"

"I thought you said you were going to get a job."

"I tried. It's not easy. And my papers aren't in order so I have to do it illegally."

"Just so you know, I've got a big day tomorrow. Sheila's daughter Allsion is getting married, and I am helping her with the wedding, and your brother's in the wedding party. The last thing I need to do is to have to go traipsing off to wire you money. As if I already didn't have enough to do."

"I know, Mommy. Thank you, you're a dear. I love you. Send it to the same place as before."

"I love you too. Now piss off and goodnight."

She sent it before coming here, after she went over to Laurie's to borrow white sling-back shoes, and Susan's to borrow a white mohair shawl for the wedding.

Lily holds up the next dress. It's a soft green, fresh and summery, with a hint of yellow in the lime, and with plain lines, nothing too drastic or froufrou.

"Excuse me, Ma'am," Brittany calls from outside the change room. "Is there something I can take away?"

"Oh please don't call me ma'am, dearie. Makes me feel ancient. Call me Lily."

"You're not old! Have you forgotten what I told you before?"

The dresses she's tried on lay on the floor. She'll have to reach down to pick them up, then pass them over the change room door. She doesn't want to, but Brittany has her work to do and she shouldn't hold her back. Her hips, arms, back and knees ache as she gathers the dresses and passes them over.

"Will there be dancing at the wedding?" Brittany asks.

"There'll be a DJ." Sheila's nephew was in charge of music.

"Don't forget to take your dancing shoes."

Once they were done in the kitchen tonight, Lily and Sheila would have a few drinks, kick off their shoes and dance. She'll pay for it tomorrow, but she doesn't care; a person has to have a little fun. Lily does a hip wiggle and a little two-step in front of the mirror.

She felt something then, a sensation around her hips and legs. Her panties lay bunched at her bare feet. She bends down to pull them up and sees the head of the safety pin has fallen off. Is there anything else left to break? She stuffs her panties into her purse.

She'll make Ben dance with her. Oh, she could wring his neck. That face of his, all purple and blue, it'll peer out of Allison's wedding pictures forever. Unless Allison's marriage doesn't last; so many don't. Lily's not looking forward to what Sheila's going to say about Ben's appearance and she'll be very direct with Lily about how she feels, as if Lily was the one who smashed his face in.

Lily let out a moan, her hands falling to her sides and the lime green dress slides to the floor. Smashed face. Chrissy comes to her when she least expects it, and with her the whole incident as if it just happened. That beautiful face, the blood matting in her blond curls. If only she had paid attention. If only she hadn't gone to the church to help with Christmas hampers, something Nick's mother got her doing because it impressed the other church ladies how her family rallied around her. She didn't even like Lily.

Lily wipes her tears with her T-shirt and sniffs. "If only, if only, if only. The story of my life."

"Is anything grabbing you?" Brittany calls.

Lily tries to speak, but emotion bunches in her throat. She coughs and manages a raspy, "I'm getting there."

Ten years ago and still, whenever she thinks about that night, she has no resistance. It's true she thinks of her less now that Ben's gone. Looking at him was like looking at Chrissy, though they weren't identical twins.

Chrissy stayed late at the school to help with the play. As usual, Lily was running late. Her dryer broke so she went to the Laundromat, and she had a couple of errands to run, a stop at the grocery store to buy a bag of Cheezies. She had a craving. It only took five minutes. Chrissy stood on the steps waiting for her, her shoulders hunched against the wind. It was snowing. The school doors had to be locked, Chrissy told her when she slid into the front sent, resentment in her voice due to her mother's lateness.

"Chrissy, listen to this song. I love this song. This was the first song your Dad and I danced to on our wedding night."

"No, Mom, I want to tell you something. Please, never mind the radio now. I know the song."

"We were at the Steer and Stein, the only two on the dance floor. Just listen and then you can tell me what's on your mind."

The two of them fought with the dial, pushing at each other, and Lily didn't see the truck coming. She didn't come to a complete stop. The roads were icy.

She has three other children. She had to go on, had to. But there were times when she thought she wouldn't.

Brittany's hand dangles a brown dress with splashes of leopard print over the door. "Not sure how you feel about animal prints, but I think this color is good for you, too. It matches your hair."

She's always liked browns, especially if she has a bit of a tan. Once, she practically lived in a brown bikini when she and Nick were first married, when they had nothing and spent months at a time in the Caribbean. She baked up like a berry, though she's never understood that expression. Berries are red, mostly. They caught their own seafood, traded labor for fruit, vegetables and meat. Nick did odd jobs, physical ones, she did housework and child care. They looked like foreigners when they came back to Canada. Nick couldn't keep his hands off her. "My Liz, my Liz," he whispered in her hair, his breath warm on her neck.

The accident. The song whose name she can't remember. Lindsay, Ben and Peter say she marks all time by the accident, but she has every right to, it was a turning point.

"Anything working?" Brittany calls.

"So far the green is the best. The brown reminds me of the Caribbean."

"Try this," Brittany's bracelets jangle as she waves an aqua colored dress in the air. "Any more dresses to pass back?"

Lily hands over a couple. "These are definite no's. I'll hang on to the maybes. Two so far." She supposes she should look at the prices before she decides on one. "This aqua is the color of the Caribbean Sea."

She presses the dress into her nose, breathes in, hoping to recapture the smell of the sea, feel the warmth of the strong trade winds. With lobster butter dripping from their fingers they promised to love each other forever. They leaned forward for greasy kisses in the booth at the back of the Steer and Stein. Before the four children came along, when all they knew to expect from each other was joy, when it seemed that was all life had to offer.

After the accident, he looked at her differently. "Were you drinking coffee? Putting on makeup? Talking on the cell? Or were you just not paying attention, like you usually do, talking a mile a minute."

She'd shut up for the rest of her life if it would bring Chrissy back. The therapist said it would take a long time to heal, but there could be no healing, especially in the face of his blame; only a slow, corrosive sense of self-hatred.

Whenever the whim took him, he left, spontaneous, on the spur of the moment, gave her no explanation, no notice, escaping the daily reminders of Chrissy, of all of them. Went with his buddies to golf in Florida, hunt in the north, fish on Lake Nipissing, leaving to deliberately forget while she was home tending to the sorrow. And when she had a chance to go and see her mother in California, what did she find when she got back?

"Black and white is very classy," Brittany's arm waves the dress over the top of the door. "And this one has a built-in bra and a very sexy plunging back."

Lily smirks. Classy is beyond her means or position in life, but she might as well try it on. Why not? as Brittany says. "It's nice." You're a very patient, caring person, Brittany."

"I'm here to help, that's my job." Lily's compliment put a brightness in Brittany's voice.

Lily slips off her bra, drapes it on a hook, and looks at the dress: a black and white geometric pattern on top, a solid black skirt. Black and white. There it was when she got back from California, came home in the middle of the afternoon and a week early, expecting to find no one. And in her bedroom, the two of them. She ran downstairs and threw up in the kitchen sink. Right under her nose, he'd been carrying on with her neighbor, the woman who refused to say hello when they met on garbage night and Lily decided she just wasn't the friendly type.

Nick came into the kitchen buttoning his shirt, his feet bare, his hair disheveled. "So, now you know. It's over, Lily. It's so over." The front door closed.

Somehow she probably knew, but she didn't want to admit it or face it, resisting the change that came with it. Her life had already changed so much. "Get out!"

She wouldn't bother with the black and white dress. You have to be able to strut in a dress with such a dramatic plunging back, wear it with a certain panache that projects elegance and class and confidence. She'd feel weighed down by pretence.

The tears well up again. She's such a jellyfish when it comes to special events, they always make her emotional, but today she is out of control. Allison and Chrissy were the same age. That's how she met Sheila—the two girls played together. It could be *her* daughter getting married today. Sheila and her husband Don could be Lily and Nick standing by Chrissy's side. She must snap out of it or she'll be useless to Sheila, to everyone.

She will try the lime green on again and thinks this could well be the one. It's that spring green she likes, the color of new leaves bursting from a tree, or shoots pushing up through the earth; a color of promise, of beautiful things still to come.

A buzz comes from inside her purse. Ben's phone is ringing. "Where are you?" Sheila asks.

"I'm getting a dress for the wedding. I won't be much longer."

"Getting a dress? *Now*?"

"Yes, I know, I know. But you know how I am. I didn't have anything to wear and I didn't have time before." Sheila knew she didn't go to fancy events and wouldn't have anything appropriate hanging in her closet, or in one of her piles.

"I'm at the church, and I don't see the flowers. The service starts in twenty minutes." Sheila's voice is shrill. "Tell me you did get them! Tell me!"

"Oh my god," Lily screams. "I forgot. There's just been so much today. Money to Peter in England and Thunder underfoot, and I had to get my hair done and to go to Laurie's to borrow her shoes and Susan's for a shawl. I'll go, I'll go. I'm going right now. Tell the minister to wait fifteen minutes. He won't mind."

"No, Lily. I am not going to do that. This will not be on your terms. This is my daughter's wedding and you are not going to delay it one minute." Sheila sounds hysterical and Lily wonders why do weddings do this to the mother of the bride? She's gone over the top.

"You know, Sheila, I've been helping you. I'm trying to help you save money. I've decorated and I'm working in the kitchen tonight. The least you can do is give me fifteen minutes. That's all I'm asking."

"You and your confounded sense of time. You know darn well you'll be longer than fifteen minutes. What am I supposed to tell the guests? Or Allison? This is *her* day!" Sheila is sobbing and seems to be talking to herself. "I don't know what to do. This is a real mess. I'll have to get Don involved, and you know what he's like. You know what, Lily? Don't come. Stay away. I don't want another one of your mix ups. You are not welcome." Sheila hangs up.

Lily stares at the phone. Not welcome? After all she's done? How can that be? She loves weddings, and Ben is in it. They'll have a dance later tonight. Surely she should be allowed to see him? After all her help, this is what she gets? Sheila's just being over sensitive. She's overtired, overexcited. She'll change her mind. Lily will get the flowers after the service and take them to the reception hall and place them around and they'll be beautiful and no one will even notice they were missing at the church.

Here's what she knows: if she doesn't show up for the wedding, if she does what Sheila told her to do in her hysterical state, Sheila will only feel terrible later, after she calms down, when she remembers telling Lily to stay away. Lily must go so Sheila won't ruin her own day.

If she hurries she can catch the end of the service, and maybe they won't start on time. These things shouldn't, lots of people are late, not just her. She'll tell Brittany what's happened, how she's lost track of time, and she'll take the lime green dress, but could she please ring it up quickly? She looks at the tag. Much more than what she wanted to spend, but she's left it too late and now she has no choice. She was late for her own wedding.

The name of the song comes out of nowhere and lands in her thoughts, wedges itself there, holds back all other thoughts, takes her breath away. "Brittany," she calls, and pulls the latch on the door, steps out into the bright room. Several shoppers turn towards her.

Brittany is over at the cash register and her mouth falls open when she sees Lily. She shouts "Just a minute" to the woman she is serving at the cash register, also turning this way, and rushes towards Lily. She wraps her arms around her and whispers in Lily's ear. "I will cover you until we back into the change room. You're not wearing a stitch."

"I remember," Lily whispers. It is as if she is having the first dance all over again, but with Brittany now, her body pressing into Lily's, warm and human and comfortable and caring, as they moved steadily backwards. She wraps her arms more tightly around Brittany and tells her, "You've been such a help. I remember the name, it came back to me. It was *All of Me*. Do you know it? It goes like this." Lily sings softly into Brittany's ear. *"All of me, why not take all of me."*

Brittany says, "I don't know why you are singing or what you are talking about. Right now I need to get you covered again."

About the author:

Catharine Leggett lives in London, Ontario, Canada. Her short stories have appeared in a number of print and online journals, including, Room, Event, The Antigonish Review,The New Quarterly, Canadian Author, paperbytes, as well as on CBC Radio. Her novel, "The Way to Go Home", was a finalist in the Columbus Creative Cooperative Great Novel Contest for 2013. A short story, a finalist for the Eric Hoffer Short Fiction Award, appears in Best New Writing 2014. A short story is forthcoming in the Main Street Rag Law and Disorder anthology.

DISMISSED
©2014 by Ronna L. Edelstein

The treadmill is not working its usual magic. It is not transporting Vera out of the reality of her life into the hypnotic world filled only with the rhythmic repetition of moving feet. Even the large television that entertains all the exercisers in her section seems to be mocking Vera. Someone turned the channel to a repeat of a recent *Phil Donahue Show* and Phil's guest of the day—an omniscient, omnipresent shrink who crawls into people's psyches and souls to make them better. Vera knows, however, that neither Phil nor his guest would be welcoming her into the therapeutic television studio, or healing office complete with couch and easily accessible tissues. She fears that both the talk show host and doctor, despite their power and high rate of success, lack the knowledge and ability to help her.

Vera increases her speed, but her rapid jogging on the swiftly moving mat fails to delete the events of the day before from Vera's mind. Nothing about the beginning of yesterday had prepared Vera for the day's malignant end—an experience that, she knew, would forever scar her.

She had followed her school day routine by getting up early; not even Homer's rosy-fingered dawn had yet awakened. The still snoring sun snuggled in her soft cloud, oblivious to the yawns of the Man-in-the-Moon and the dimming twinkle of the tired stars. Only the night people—the trash collectors, the doctors and nurses who never sleep, and the bakers eager to heat up their ovens—had left the comfort of their beds. Only the night people and Vera.

Vera loves this time before dawn. It wraps her like the quilt that she inherited after Grandma died. Within its comforting cocoon, Vera reflects and reminisces before facing the challenges and enjoying the rewards of whatever lies ahead. Yesterday her thoughts had taken her back to when she was a little girl and had played school with her family of dolls, when she was a high school student and had served as the president of Future Teachers of America, and when she was a graduate student earning her Master's degree in teaching. Teaching had become a dream fulfilled—not a broken dream of marriage ending in divorce, of motherhood often descending into a "Mommy Dearest" scenario.

Yesterday—the third Friday in June—marked a milestone for Vera: the completion of her first year of teaching after spending decades raising her children while longing for a return to the classroom. Since before Labor Day, she had met daily with almost a hundred eighth graders; some from trailer parks and some from mansions overlooking lakes, but all sharing the up-one-moment and down-the-next personality of teenagers. For almost ten months, Vera had nourished those students with books and words, and she had nurtured them with every ounce of caring she possessed. Now, as she prepared to send her eighth graders off to high school, she felt a sense of pride for the almost-adults her students had become, and a sense of loss for the emptiness their leaving would create.

The sweat, like a miniature waterfall, pours down Vera's face. She staggers off the treadmill and heads to the elliptical, yet another Inquisition machine that the health club trainers delude her into embracing as an ally in her goal to get fit. Happily, the repetitive motion of the machine lulls Vera; she drifts into her imagination where bullying does not exist, where pleasure does not become pain. She relives the early hours of yesterday, the time when the pendulum hung in mid-air and had not yet decided to swing in a way that would inflict harm upon Vera.

As always, Vera had been the second to arrive at school; only the custodian had come earlier. Even if he had not turned on the lights, Vera could have found her way from the parking lot to her classroom. She followed the sweet aroma of chocolate chip cookies still lingering from the Home Economics kitchen to the more pungent smells of paints, oils, and dyes emanating from the art room. She passed the choir room where, if she listened carefully, she could hear the echoes of the eighth grade chorus practicing its songs of friendship for the commencement ceremony. A sharp right turn took Vera past the Media Center, her favorite room in the school, where computers and books shared a peaceful coexistence. Another right turn ended in her classroom.

Once a place of vibrant posters encouraging students to "Read a Book—Make a Friend" and "Put It In Writing," and bulletin boards, like a large family refrigerator, displaying the work of imaginative minds, her classroom now looked like a winter home abandoned for a summer cottage. Books wrapped in plastic bags filled the shelves, bits of chalk lay amid piles of chalk dust, and Vera's desk, usually crowded with pens, pencils, staplers, papers, and other school paraphernalia, lay bare.

The elliptical, grinding to a halt, paroles Vera from her thirty minutes of imprisonment. She decides to next conquer the Stairmaster. Vera has always liked that machine because it reminds her of the crystal staircase in Langston Hughes' poem, "Mother to Son." Despite a marriage that never began with "once upon a time" or ended "happily ever after" and despite a life spent more in the pursuit than the fulfillment of happiness, Vera once believed that one day her stepping and climbing would take her to the top—to the highest landing where everything will be as smooth as a crystal stair. Today, however, she knows differently; yesterday her students reminded her that her life is not a crystal staircase but—like the mother's in the poem—is one with torn-up boards, sharp tacks, and painful splinters. Vera had spent the past year trying to polish and smooth the stairs through teaching her students to embrace the "stand in another person's shoes to understand, not judge" lesson of her favorite book, *To Kill a*

Mockingbird, through rewarding her students' writing efforts by typing and compiling class literary journals, through reminding her students that they were special. Yet, with one act, her eighth graders had shoved her to the bottom of the stairs.

Friday's commencement ceremony had been flawless. Even the class clowns had understood the seriousness of the occasion and had not turned the assembly into a circus. At first, Vera had not recognized some of her students. The boys, often dressed in jeans that hung too low on their hips, now wore dress pants and shirts with collars; the girls looked demure in their dresses and low-heeled shoes. No one booed when the principal called the name of a less popular student, although a few boys did whistle when one of the more attractive—and developed—girls walked across the stage to receive her certificate.

The students had marched into the gym to the school band's playing of "Pomp and Circumstance." No one minded the band's occasional off-key notes; instead, the pomp of the occasion had a calming effect, as if the students sensed that the circumstance—the transition from middle school to high school—deserved a response of dignity. The eighth graders were replacing silliness with seriousness, devilry with dedication, because college and adulthood seemed less distant than they had the day before. Grades would matter for that all-important GPA, extracurricular involvement would enhance resumes, and roads taken or not taken would affect ultimate destinations. Vera, confident that she had given her students what they needed to succeed, observed how her students sat straighter, fussed less, and listened more closely to the speeches delivered by peers and school staff.

Once the formal ceremony ended, the students and their families gathered around long tables filled with cookies, punch, pictures, and a huge sheet cake that encouraged the graduates to "Make a Difference." Vera slipped out of the gym, knowing she would have time at the end of the day to say good-bye. She had written a poem for her students—a summary of the year's Language Arts curriculum, projects, and high points—and printed a copy for each student on rainbow-colored paper. Just as she had welcomed her students in September with a package of M&Ms for a "sweet" year, so did she attach a package of M&Ms to each poem for a "sweet" future.

The rest of the afternoon had passed in a flurry of "have a great summer" wishes and Hollywood-like air kisses from one colleague to another. Vera had stopped to chat with a handful of seventh graders gathered in front of a row of green lockers; many of these boys and girls would become her students when the new year began. The group seemed rather benign, except for one girl whose eyes dissected Vera as if looking for flaws to mock. Although Vera refused to let the girl diminish the joy of the day, she did silently pray that the impersonal school computer would assign the girl to the other eighth grade Language Arts teacher.

At the end of the day, Vera had met with all of her eighth graders in the gym for a special time of camaraderie. After she distributed her poem and candy gift, one student flicked the lights and another shouted for silence; Vera did not initially understand what was happening. Then, a group of four students approached her: Justin, the jock of eighth grade whose muscles—and cockiness—promised him success on the high school football team and in the social arena; Courtney, the golden girl whose Barbie doll looks belied her insightful, acute mind; Seth, the intellect whose willingness to help classmates achieve academic success made him more hero than nerd; and Caitlin, the diminutive mascot whose dimples and wide-eyed innocence ensured she would garner the protection and respect of her peers.

Justin handed Vera a flat present wrapped in the golden colors of her favorite bookstore. It was a hardback version of *To Kill a Mockingbird*. The students had teased Vera for using a tattered paperback copy of the core class novel that Vera kept in a plastic bag in order to keep the pages from scattering like fall leaves. As Vera oohed and aahed over the book, the entire eighth grade applauded. Hearing their accolades—For her? For the book? For both?—made Vera smile. She was convinced that she and Harper

Lee, the author, had found the words to end prejudice and all acts of discrimination.

Once the students had settled down, Courtney approached Vera and gave her a glittery bag filled with red pens. "Use these to 'bleed' over the papers of next year's eighth graders," Courtney joked. Seth quickly handed Vera a super-sized bag of M&Ms. "So you can fill your lunch yogurt container with sweetness," he said.

Only Caitlin remained. She waited until the students clapped their hands and stamped their feet in a drum roll beat before presenting Vera with a beautifully wrapped box. "This is a very special gift from us to you," Caitlin announced. Vera, so shocked by yet another present, did not hear the laughter from some students or notice the eye rolling mirth of others.

Huffing and puffing like the nemesis of the three little pigs, Vera continues her climb to reach the top of the Stairmaster, an effort as futile as her hope that what lay inside the beautifully wrapped box had been an illusion, not a reality. As Vera finally heads to the women's locker room to shower, she passes the gym where women and men engage in an intensive dance aerobics class. Vera stops, presses her forehead against the glass, and watches the svelte women and buff men sway and shake to the music. They all seem free, as if immune to the problems that inundate Vera. She wonders if any of them has a life rooted in self-hatred and the mockery of others. Vera, using her forehead to create a soft tattoo against the glass, thinks of an old television commercial for toothpaste that placed an invisible shield in front of a beaming child. That shield, like the toothpaste, was supposed to prevent decay from eroding the child's mouth. Vera wishes she could erect that shield now—that she could have erected it yesterday before opening the gift.

With students crowding around her, Vera carefully unwrapped the blue and white ribbon, wondering if the students had deliberately chosen the colors of the school as a special way to honor her. She removed the tape holding together the silver paper and gingerly lifted the lid of the box. Inside a bed of silver tissue paper sat a porcelain figure—a beaver dressed as a professor with a cap on its head and a ruler in its hand. Yet, the beaver's most prominent feature was its teeth—two large protruding front teeth, mirror images of those that had defined Vera's mouth for decades.

Vera stared at the beaver, oblivious to the giggling and whistling of the students. She wanted to believe the gift was a tribute to her teaching, was her students' way of acknowledging that she had made a difference in their lives. But one look at the sea of students told her differently. She became Carrie at the prom, standing under a waterfall of blood; she was Simon in *Lord of the Flies,* surrounded by children-turned-savages who wanted to "kill the beast;" she was the piece of chalk that could transform a blank board into poetry, but now lay broken in half and pulverized into unrecognizable pieces.

Vera managed to mumble a thank you just as the principal's voice boomed on the loud speaker: "Have a good summer! Dismissed!" The word "dismissed" bounced from one wall to another, not stopping until it found its final resting place deep within the soul of Vera.

Vera enters the gym's shower, lathers herself with soap, and scrubs the sagging breasts, flapping underarms, and protruding stomach that defy her hours on the treadmill, elliptical, and Stairmaster. She stays under the water until the spray turns cold. Fearing that the club manager will raise her dues to pay for her extended time in the shower, she reluctantly leaves the safety of the curtained cubicle, dries herself with one of the club's yellowed towels, dresses, and heads to her car.

She starts to drive home, but then makes a U-turn that takes her around two lakes and one park back to the school. The usually crowded parking lot now holds only a few trucks belonging to the cleaning crew. These men and women have already begun the tedious process of preparing the school for the fall semester by removing gum stuck to chairs, emptying lockers of moldy bread and remnants of tuna, and gathering scraps of papers that once contained the solutions to math problems or the promise of an engaging story.

Vera enters the school, heads to her classroom, opens the bottom desk drawer, and confronts the beaver. The two engage in a staring contest—a competition that Vera loses. She closes her eyes and rubs her fingers over the beaver's porcelain cap. The sharp edges of the cap knick her skin and cause a trickle of blood to flow from her finger onto the beaver. Vera smiles, glad that the beaver at least bears superficial signs of the pain that she feels. The ruler in the beaver's hand looks ominous—like the one Mr. Simon, Vera's sixth grade science teacher, had used to slap her palm when she dared to talk without raising her hand and waiting to be called on. Mr. Simon, who had liked Vera, had not hit her hard, but the sting from the slap had lasted throughout the decades. Now, Vera would opt for hundreds of Mr. Simon slaps to avoid the piercing sting coming from the beaver gift.

Finally, she opens her eyes and looks at the beaver's teeth: two rectangular pieces the size of miniature erasers that begin in the beaver's upper gums and extend almost to the beaver's chin. Had Rachel, the shy eighth grader who blossomed when she won first place in a contest Vera had encouraged her to enter, contributed money towards this gift? Had Lindsey and Haley, best friends who needed no one else to feel popular, given money without thinking about all the Dairy Queens Vera had treated them to for a job well-done? Vera thinks of all the students for whom she had written congratulatory postcards, had sent "thinking of you" notes, or had extended deadlines due to an "I'm having a bad day" excuse. Did these students participate in the selection and buying of the beaver? Did they find joy in targeting Vera's Achilles' heel—her teeth—by choosing such a present?

The beaver sits in silence, oblivious to the wounds and scars it has created. With Vera, it listens to the ticking of the wall clock. When Vera jolts at a ringing bell—even on the first Saturday of summer vacation, the bell still rings—the beaver remains still and in control. And then Vera cries—not the soft tears that come from a sweet memory or the quick tears that come from a passing disappointment, but the heavy, hail-like tears that come from disillusionment, from a dismissal both deep and permanent. Vera senses that one of the workers has stopped outside her classroom door, but the man does not enter; maybe he understands that something private—and painful—is happening in the otherwise indifferent classroom. Maybe he realizes that any intrusion on his part will shatter the fragile woman sitting at the teacher's desk, sobbing as she clutches a porcelain figure in her hands.

Vera clenches the beaver and remembers the little children—friends of her son and daughter—who, too young to know that name-calling can hurt more than sticks and stones, had teased her about her overbite. She remembers a close adult friend stumbling over her words when she once suggested that Vera get braces. And she remembers a crude man, an acquaintance of her then husband, wondering aloud what it would be like to kiss a woman with such unattractive teeth. Yet, Vera had always thought that the classroom, the one place where her intelligence and creativity mattered more than her tallness and teeth—her tall teeth—would save her from such uncaring words and cruel looks. The porcelain beaver proves Vera wrong.

The room, always a hub of activity, now seems like an empty box. Girls, representing the different groups within eighth grade—the readers and writers, the fashion mavens, the would-be dancers and Broadway stars—do not huddle in different corners to eat their lunch, chat, and giggle. The handful of students who received detention from another teacher do not slump in their chairs and try to ignore Vera's eyes as they write their "I'm sorry" essays, and she alternates between grading essays and looking at them with concern. The conflicted ones, those still in the process of figuring out who they are and where they belong, do not nibble at their lunch as they reflect and regroup in Vera's room. All year, Vera had welcomed these students; she had opened her door to them. Now, thanks to the beaver, she wonders if everything has been a sham—that the world she thought she had built on nurturing and nourishing had instead been a world with neither roots nor respect.

Before leaving the classroom, Vera places the beaver in her purse. Once in the car, she sits it on the passenger seat and wraps the seatbelt around its portly stomach. She contemplates throwing it into the woods or drowning it in the lake or even returning it to the store to buy something less malignant. Yet, she knows that she will keep it—maybe tucking it behind her pajamas at the back of the drawer or maybe sitting it atop her printer. She will keep it as a reminder that a once-upon-a-time school year does not guarantee a happily-ever-after final dismissal day.

Vera drives home, steering along a road that is a concrete treadmill; it will not only move her forward towards her apartment and summer, but, when fall arrives, it will also take her back to her classroom and the teenagers who occupy her life.

Although the setting sun creates a dazzling light in the sky, its rays dismiss Vera, leaving her face hidden in shadow. Instead, the sun spotlights the beaver, giving its porcelain skin a luminous glow. The beaver, oblivious to Vera, smiles its toothy grin.

About the author:

I am a lifelong learner and teacher, a mother and daughter, and an avid reader and fan of theatre. Whether teaching writing at the University of Pittsburgh or sitting with my 97-year-old father in the park, I try to find meaning and beauty in the world around me—and in those who inhabit it.

I thank all the organizations and individuals who have honored me as a writer. These include Scribes Valley Publishing for recognizing all five (and counting) of my "Vera" stories; Dream Quest One for awarding me first place for my essay, "Lovingly Ever After;" First Line Anthology for including my book review and story in its magazine; and the editors of the Pittsburgh Post-Gazette for consistently choosing my memoirs and essays for Page Two or the Op-Ed Page.

THE WHITE CARPET
©2014 by I O Kirkwood

Ten months without his shouting and his hurtful fists had been like a spa retreat. Suddenly, the vacation was over. I had come home from school and found myself returned to a nightmare. The situation reminded me of a dream last night about hordes of little black spiders that crawled along the ceiling, promising in tinny falsettos to devour my mother and siblings.

I had that dream at least once a month and the outcome hadn't changed. I would chase the dark mass of spiders through the sleeping house; their shrieks of delight fueling my panic as I met empty bed after empty bed. Not even bones were left behind.

I studied the wet coffee grounds as they soaked into the white carpet. My mother loved that carpet. She guarded it jealously; it was one of the few nice things that she owned. I mourned its ruin more than I did the beating to come. She would be angry with me. She was *always* angry with me.

"Why can't you do anything right?" my father said.

He faced me with an expression that darkened his eyes with violent promise; he expected an answer and I had none. My heart beat a sharp tattoo against my breast. I tasted the metal of my fear. In my mind, I starred in another of my recurring nightmares: I swung my fists, I fought back, but I moved in slow motion and my muscles felt too weak to land an effective defense. My unseen opponent was much faster than I.

My anger was so large, I usually crumbled before it. The fear of pain blotted out any foothold in reason I had obtained in quieter moments. I only knew how to turn tail and run.

He pressed his advantage. "I can't leave you alone for a moment. I come home, expecting a welcome, and the only thing here to greet me is a sink full of dishes and garbage. Is it too much to expect gratitude? You can't even take out the damn trash without making a mess!"

Any other time I would have cried. I looked at the wreckage of the paper bag that had dumped its contents onto the carpet. The earthy scent of damp compost imprinted on my mind. It occurred to me that the person who had used a paper grocery bag for trash was more to blame than I.

My eyes narrowed. I was thirteen now. I'd had my first menses this past summer. I had spent the last ten months unmolested, able to move without fear of corporal reprisal for a dropped towel or a forgotten dish. I was able to pursue activities that pleased me: Word-A-Day, listening to music on my headphones, and having friends over without worrying about...an episode.

Sending my father away had been one of the kindest things my mother had ever done. Inviting him back was the worst of betrayals. I had stood on the landing only minutes before, listening to his curses, and had hated her with a violence that still surprised me.

"No more." My words echoed in a silence pregnant with shock.

My father stood there, his hands loose at his sides, and gaped at me. "What?"

I waited for the fists to land, but he frowned as if I had learned the trick of pulling my thumb off or how to whistle without his guidance. I thought of the times, all too infrequent but precious, when he had laughed with me, his moments of kindness, and I dragged in a breath.

"Maybe if you stopped yelling at me for once—stopped hitting me—I *could* do something right!"

His gaze turned inward. He frowned and then lifted his hand. Instead of cowering, I thrust my chin forward and met his eyes. I dared him to strike me, but his palm pressed against his forehead and wiped down his face. His other hand went to his hip. He was in no position to swing.

He sighed, "You're right. I'm sorry."

I didn't believe him at first, but then he turned away. Relief dragged at my limbs even though a tiny part of me waited for him to fly into a rage. The trash still lay on the rug and I bent down to gather it.

"You will never touch me again." My voice overrode the clank of dishes. The running water silenced and I cringed inwardly. Plastic rustled and his footsteps shook the floor. I started to rise. If I was going to get a beating, I would take it standing.

A plastic garbage bag dangled in front of my face, "Get up as much as you can and I'll take care of the stain, okay?"

Silence was acceptance. That was the rule. For once, I had spoken and he was silent.

I took the garbage bag and dropped my head. My fingers were coated in coffee grounds and eggshells. Tears burned at the corners of my eyes; relief coursed in heady bliss through my veins. In my head I chanted, "One nightmare down."

The sense of liberation was like sucking in air after staying under water too long. I hadn't realized I was holding my breath. Even for the ten months he was gone, I had held my breath.

This victory, this battle won, was the beginning of my own personal war. I made a vow. I was going behind enemy lines. I would go deep into my dreams, and I would retrieve my POWs from the nightmare spiders. I would swing and my arms and legs would move faster than my opponent's. My fists would connect and I would overcome, silent no more.

About the author:

I.O. Kirkwood, wordsmith-storyteller-alternate historian-metal junkie, resides near Charm City, USA. In between bouts of banging her head, blogging, and twittering, she's also the author of Subatomic Revolt, volume 2 in Mike Lynch's No Revolution Is Too Big series.

www.ingramcontent.com/pod-product-compliance
Lightning Source LLC
Chambersburg PA
CBHW071453030726
47593CB00003B/988